My Cousin's Keeper

My Cousin's Keeper

Simon French

CANDLEWICK PRESS

Copyright © 2012 by Simon French

First U.S. edition 2014

Library of Congress Catalog Card Number 2013953539
ISBN 978-0-7636-6279-0

14 15 16 17 18 19 BVG 10 9 8 7 6 5 4 3 2

Printed in Berryville, VA, U.S.A.

This book was typeset in Adobe Garamond Pro.

Candlewick Press
99 Dover Street
Somerville, Massachusetts 02144

visit us at www.candlewick.com

For Quinn Wen Tian

We're brothers, we are.

That's what he had said. Suddenly, his arm was around my shoulder as we knelt together on my bedroom floor, surrounded by most of my toys. He had looked up at my mom as she held her camera to take the photo, and that's exactly what came out of his mouth when the camera flash went off. In the photo, he was smiling, although his eyes didn't seem to. In the photo, my mouth was open and I looked a little surprised.

In truth, I remembered being angry. This boy, who I didn't know, had snuck away from everybody else in our backyard and found my bedroom. He had found all my toys as well, and by the time I discovered him, nearly everything I liked and played with was spread across my bedroom.

"This is my room," I had told him. "Leave my things alone!" And I had knelt down to start gathering up my favorite things. Mom had appeared in the doorway at that moment and taken the photo, not realizing how annoyed I was.

Afterward, I had shaken the boy's arm away from my shoulder and said in amazement, "I'm not your brother. I don't even know you."

"You should have asked Kieran first," Mom told the boy gently. "This is Kieran's room, and these are his things." And to me, she added, "*Is* there something you don't mind him playing with, Kieran?" Then she reminded me who this stranger was. It was Bon, my cousin. "He's our guest, and I want you to look after him a little," Mom instructed.

But I didn't want him in my room, and I didn't want to be anywhere near him. He had said something completely strange and untrue. He had even *hugged* me. Bon was nearly the same age as me; I already knew that. For a moment I studied his face to see if there *was* any kind of resemblance. "I don't want you in here. Go away," I muttered.

Bon looked at me blankly, as though I had spoken another language. Up close, he smelled a little of sweat and pee. His shirt was faded and coming apart at the edges, and his socks showed through the torn tips of his sneakers. His hair was longer than mine, and it was tied back into a blond ponytail. He wasn't the sort of cousin I had expected, and I didn't know why he and his mom had suddenly turned up at my dad's birthday barbecue. And Mom was surprised to see her older sister after so many years.

Later in the evening, after lots of people had left and it was mostly Dad's soccer friends gathered around the last of the beer and food, Mom said to me, "Kieran, you know that was probably the most toys your cousin had ever laid eyes on in his life."

"I don't care," I grumbled. "He just came in and touched everything without asking. He wasn't even invited in the first place."

"It wasn't his fault," Mom answered. "None of us had any idea Bon and Renee would show up."

Dad's birthday barbecue had begun in the usual way. Nan had been at our house and in the kitchen almost right after breakfast, helping Mom prepare party snacks and salads. Early afternoon, the neighbors strolled over from next door, and then our friends from around town, with their kids. A couple of Dad's work friends from Rural Engineering arrived together, and as our backyard began to fill up, the talk and laughter grew louder and louder. A lot of us kids climbed through the wire strands of the back fence to play games on the strip of grass that ran along behind the houses in our street—except for some of the little girls who

3

stayed in the backyard to play with my sister, Gina.

When most of Dad's soccer team arrived, the noise got even louder. The season wasn't due to start for another two weeks, so a long afternoon and a late night wasn't going to affect a weekend game. As cooking smells from the barbecue began to drift across to where we played in the back, the team sang Dad a funny and rude birthday song. Even Nan laughed.

And then someone else arrived. I couldn't remember Aunt Renee, but at first I wanted to like her. She was so unlike Mom, a different shape and size, with a louder way of speaking. She dressed differently from Mom, too: in a leather jacket, jeans, and black buckled boots. The man she had brought with her was dressed much the same. I didn't take a lot of notice of Bon, because I was more interested in my aunt's jacket and the tattoo I could see peeking out from under her sleeve. Mom and Nan walked over to say hello and give my aunt a kiss, but Mom's voice sounded a bit awkward as she made some introductions to the people nearest.

"We were just traveling through," my aunt said. "If we'd known there was a birthday happening, we would have brought something."

"Good to see you again, Renee," my nan said, not sounding as though she meant it. "It's been a while." Already I had seen her lean over to kiss Bon, and now she held him close, hugging him so that, for a few moments at least, he was unable to move.

"God, this one's grown," my aunt remarked, pointing at me. "Kieran, isn't it? Last time I saw him he was just about still in diapers."

"Bon's grown up a lot, too," Mom answered. "It's been far too long since we've seen you both." But my aunt was already busy showering attention on Gina and saying how pretty she looked. I knew it was the first time she had ever seen my little sister.

I had heard Aunt Renee talked about, mostly when adults thought I hadn't been listening. She was my mom's older sister, quite a bit older, and I remembered that some of the Christmas cards Mom had mailed her had come back with a RETURN TO SENDER stamp on them. My aunt seemed to move a lot.

I asked Mom quietly if the man my aunt had brought along to Dad's birthday was my uncle. "No, definitely not!" she told me.

Nan had a photo of Bon, just the one. It was a baby photo, kept on her fridge door, in a colorful magnetic frame. I'd often looked at that photo and wondered about the cousin I didn't know.

Bon hadn't followed us kids back out to the grassy strip after we'd come in to raid the food. He poked around our backyard and seemed a bit lost at first, but then went and stood with Gina and her little friends. When I saw him next, he was over at the food table, busily eating handfuls of chips, crackers, and dips. He spent quite a bit of time doing this, and I wondered if he was being greedy or was just really hungry.

Then I heard my aunt's voice. "Are you listening to me?" It was unexpectedly loud and angry, and I looked over in time to see her with one hand clenched around Bon's face. Her fingers pressed tightly into his cheeks so that his mouth opened a little.

Aunt Renee looked furious. "I told you to behave," she said through clenched teeth. All our guests stopped talking for a moment, and some of them looked a bit shocked. But Bon looked away from his mother as though nothing had happened. I expected him to rub his sore face, or even to cry. Instead, he gazed into space, as his shoulders and arms flopped around a little, before his mother let go of him. He said nothing.

Nan walked over and *did* say something, but my aunt replied, "No, don't tell me what to do. He's my kid."

Nan looked anxiously at Bon, then reached over and ran her hand gently across his shoulder. My aunt glared. Gradually, uncomfortably, people began to talk again, until the party found its noise and laughter once more. When I looked next, I could see Bon walking through the back door and into our house, not knowing at that moment he had been on his way to my bedroom and my toys.

We're brothers, we are.

"He said that weird thing, too," I reminded Mom.

"He's probably quite lonely," she replied. "And, quite likely, he was excited about finally meeting his cousins." Mom paused. "Thank you for letting him play with some of your things."

"I didn't *want* him to," I said. "It wasn't like he asked first." I paused and frowned. "Will they visit us again?"

Mom answered quietly. "I hope so, for Bon's sake. As for Renee . . ."

Another uncomfortable thought came back to me. "She *hurt* him." I had never seen an adult do that before. Sometimes in stores I had heard other parents yell at their kids or smack them on the hand, especially some of the teenagers who pushed strollers or led little processions of toddlers. "She was hurting him," I said again, trying to make sense of it. "His face—"

"I'm sorry you saw that," Mom said. "He wasn't being naughty; he was probably just plain hungry."

My aunt had not stayed long at our party, either. I remembered that.

"Time for us to get back on the road," the boyfriend

said after Dad had blown the candles out on his chocolate mud cake. The good-byes were brief, and the three of them left almost as unexpectedly as they had arrived. I had walked with Nan and my parents to the driveway gate to see them off, to watch the boyfriend's big black pickup take them to the end of our street and then away out of town. They had sat in the single front seat together, but my cousin, jammed in the middle, was the only one who turned and looked back. He didn't wave; he simply stared at us through the window, all the way to the corner. It was as though he had wanted to stay behind. I was glad he hadn't. Then I happened to look at Nan waving, her face looking as sad as I thought I'd ever seen it. "That poor child," she had said, her voice soft and defeated.

Later, when I began to straighten up my room, I noticed that my medieval castle had been moved. Its army of horses and knights was set out in formation across the carpet, the royal family and their wizard on the castle parapets, standing close, as though talking to one another. The castle had been a birthday gift only months before, and I was furious that it had been touched and rearranged. And then, as I frowned and muttered to myself, I discovered that two things were missing—a white horse and an armored knight, the one who carried a sword in one hand and a blue crested flag in the other. And I knew right away who had stolen them and how far away they must be by now.

This was mostly how I remembered my dad's birthday party, the year he had turned thirty-five, and the year I turned nine.

It would be two years before I saw my cousin, Bon, again.

CHAPTER

2

"Come on!" Dad called back to me. He was already halfway up the steep short hill that was Guthrie Street, his regular challenge. The way he called it back to me it sounded more like *"C'marrnn!"*—his voice heaving with the effort of his running, but also the effort of trying not to wake up everyone on the street. It was early, sometime between six thirty and seven, and this was the only thing he had said to me since we'd left home. I wanted to tell myself that it was friendly encouragement, but really I sensed he was a bit irritated at how I struggled to keep up.

C'marrnn! I could hear those two words, stretched and slurred into one, by kids and grown-ups alike, called from the sidelines of my dad's weekend games. Saturday after Saturday, we cheered and yelled as the Locomotives fought and won match points, as Dad showed his speed and skill at striking the ball into the goal. He was a fast runner, a good aimer and kicker. I was not.

But I wanted to be. I wanted to show Dad—and his noisy teammates and the kids at school—that I could do these things well. I wasn't sure what else I was particularly good at doing.

It was early in the soccer season. The day was light and the sun was already peeking above the mountains at the eastern edge of town. By midseason, it would still be dark at this time of the morning and all the streetlights would still be glowing white or orange above the stores, houses, and the park.

If I woke early enough and got my clothes and sneakers on quickly, I'd catch up with Dad at the front gate, or perhaps a little way along our street, as he began his training run. Just as often, though, he'd go without me. It always surprised me that a week's hard work in the big workshop at Rural Engineering was never enough for Dad to reward himself with a weekend of sleeping in. Early each evening, he'd leave his bicycle under the carport and walk inside, hands and clothes grimy with steel dust and oil stains. And he'd be out the next morning, jogging the streets around town, no matter how dark or cold, windy, and wet it might be. Even when soccer season finished, he would still be out running two or three times a week. But I'd get lazy, and today, after a long, burning summer and the beginnings of autumn, I was paying for missing weeks of morning runs.

Three steep streets in a row turned off Sheridan Street, just near the point where the houses stopped and the shops more or less began. More or less, because our town had once been a bigger, busier place, and there were buildings that used to be stores but that now stood empty. Sometimes I felt curious to know what might still be inside, behind the boarded-over windows, or behind old blinds and shutters.

"Come on!" Dad called once more, his voice clear and encouraging against the early-morning quiet. He was nearly at the top of the hill and I had barely begun. Guthrie was the steepest of the three streets. Fraser and Raymond were a little easier, but only just.

Today, the air was milky with fog. I could feel my face wet and cold with vapor. With all the effort and concentration I could muster, I launched myself at Guthrie Street's asphalt surface and heaved my way to the top, taking short jogging steps and keeping my eyes on my feet. I knew if I stopped halfway that the second part of the climb would feel a lot worse. Dad waited at the top, hands on his hips. Perspiration spotted his forehead and streaked down his cheeks into his beard whiskers. "Now, wasn't that fun?" He grinned. "Let's do it again!"

I dropped my mouth open to say something, but was too out of breath.

"Actually, a good place to stop for a moment," he murmured beside me, and it was true. This was the highest point in town, and you could see nearly every house and backyard. The streets straggled down to the main street and then the riverbed, the dividing line between shops and houses, between fields and the high-way to the west. I could see the silver-and-red roof of Rural Engineering, where Dad worked. After a shower and a change of clothes, he would be cycling away for a day of cutting, welding, repairing, and restoring.

The sun had climbed a tiny bit higher above the mountain range, and I let its warmth settle on my face.

"Beautiful view," he said. "I never get tired of it."

I'd heard him say this many times as we'd stood in this very spot, and sometimes I thought I could see a look in his eyes that meant he was thinking of somewhere else altogether. Because this wasn't Dad's hometown; he had come here from a bigger country town for a job he'd wanted. "Then I met your mom," he'd often say with a smile, "and the rest is history."

The view reminded me of a few things that I had

learned about living here — how in the summer, the heat turned the school playground to dust; that the winters could be numbingly cold; and that whenever it rained heavily, the street gutters quickly overflowed and had the roar of waterfalls.

Dad squished and rubbed a handful of my hair. He wasn't gentle. "You sound winded. Thought *I* was out of shape . . ."

"This street's got the toughest hill," I reminded him. "We should have started with Raymond Street and worked our way up."

"Well, I started with Raymond Street last week." He smiled. "One of the days you slept in, kiddo. You want to play on a team, then you've got to put in the training time. Hmm? No use being a bed zombie or a couch potato."

He'd used that phrase on me before, and now he ignored my shrugged shoulders, my wondering if sports were something I might only ever be average at.

"Come on," Dad said at last. "We've done the tough uphill part. Let's go downhill."

After the hill peak, Guthrie Street curved away and down to the old railroad station. No trains had run to our town for years, and there was only a museum of photos and models inside to show what a busy and important place it had once been. A couple of old restored train cars sat in the siding beside the empty platform, but at a short distance from the station, the rail lines disappeared under dirt and grass. I could keep up with Dad on the flat ground and it was a little easier now, knowing as well that we were past the halfway mark and more or less heading for home again.

We came to the very eastern end of the main street, the point where the railroad line had once led onto the old bridge and away to other towns and, eventually, the city. The bridge was wooden and had grown wobbly with age, too unsafe to walk on these days. A fence ran across at the sidewalk where the bridge began. Sometimes this was another of Dad's stopping places, but not today. As my stomach and legs began to hurt even more with the effort, he gradually got farther and farther ahead of me. Once or twice he turned to check that I was still somewhere behind him. He raised one hand in a wave, and so did I as I slowed to a walk. We would meet up at home.

The very first time we had ever run together, I had been so excited about being allowed along that I'd spent the first ten minutes telling him everything I knew about everywhere and everybody in town.

"That's the house where Lucas lives. And that's Mason's place. His brother owns that really cool car parked in the front yard. And the Imperial Hotel is where Liam's mom does the cooking. And that blue house is where Ms. Tabor, the librarian at school, lives. And—"

"Kieran!" Dad had exclaimed, his breath puffing. "This is training. You have to focus!"

Now, I stopped outside the thrift shop, where Nan volunteered several times each week. Here, she was not Nan, but Erica, the lady with the unruly dyed hair and interesting earrings. She chose the things that were displayed in the front window. She listened to local gossip and told the customers jokes. *This is my grandson Kieran and my granddaughter, Gina,* she'd tell everybody and anybody if Gina and I stopped at the shop on our walk home from school.

I never heard her mention my cousin, Bon, but sensed that she thought about him more than she ever said. By now, there was a newer photo of Bon in a frame on Nan's fridge, one taken two years before at Dad's birthday party. Once or twice, I had seen Nan lift the photo away from its frame and look at it for a long time.

I stretched my T-shirt up to wipe my forehead and then stared at my reflection in the window. My hair was flattened and wet with perspiration, my arms and legs as skinny as a stick insect's. There were other people out by now, walking their dogs and making their way in and out of the convenience store, always the first shop open in the morning. Dad was nearly a full block ahead of me, and so I began to jog again, picking up speed until I'd almost caught up with him near the corner of Sheridan Street. I could hear the light slap of his running shoes and his steady breathing.

"You caught up," he said warmly. "Well done."

I smiled. The run home would be easy.

When Mom was in a daydreaming mood, she'd talk about moving to the coast. It made me wonder what it would be like to be the new kid at school. How would it be to arrive on the playground at a new school and know absolutely nobody, or to step into a classroom and have twenty-five kids stare at me as though I were a museum exhibit? I had always lived in this town and gone to the one school, and I felt a little sorry for the new kids who arrived from time to time.

Some of them fit in and made new friends right away. Some of them looked shy and lost for days after they'd arrived; they sat alone on playground seats, or walked anxiously beside any friendly teacher that happened to be on playground duty.

I remembered one new kid who had arrived at our school, an older boy who brought his anger with him every day. For a while, he turned the playground into a battlefield, fighting other kids and being rude to the teachers. Everybody learned his name very quickly, and a gang of kids began to follow him around—which caused even more trouble. But as suddenly as he'd arrived, the boy left our school and moved on to some other place. Everyone felt relieved, and things on the playground got back to normal again.

New kids often appeared after a school break, and that was how it happened in the fall of the year I turned eleven. By the end of that first morning back at school, I knew I'd remember the date and year, because of precisely *who* the new kids were.

I saw her first, long before Mason Cutler or Lucas Xerri or any of the other boys in my class began the familiar routine of making comments loud enough for the new girl to hear once she was on the playground.

"Woo, she's a honey," remarked Lucas.

"Go on, big man," said Mason. "Go and ask her out!"

"You know where she lives?"

"Never seen her before. Go and ask her name."

"No way. You go!"

But I saw her first.

Because Gina had managed to lose not one but two school sweaters, I was rummaging through the lost and found in between the main front door and the school office. Gina had forgotten exactly where she'd left her things, and Mom had told me to go looking. The school office before class time began was always a busy place—parents dropping off notes or paying for schoolbooks or field trips, kids coming in from the playground with bleeding knees or elbows that required either a Band-Aid or a phone call home. And big brothers like me searching the lost and found for things that annoying little sisters managed to lose. Most of the usual commotion I ignored, but the front door opening and the sound of strangers' voices distracted me from my search.

They arrived in a rush, and it seemed that a private conversation hadn't quite been finished, because the mom was whispering something to the new girl, who looked annoyed and embarrassed. The two of them went to the reception desk, and I heard Mrs. Reilly, who ran the office, ask, "Yes, how can I help you?"

It was the girl who began to answer first. "I'd like to enroll, please—"

Her mom interrupted her. "I'd like to enroll my daughter, please."

I stopped rummaging and turned around. The girl had spoken as though she could hardly wait to be in a classroom full of kids she'd never met. The mom had sounded as if this were the very last place she wanted to be, and the sunglasses she wore didn't exactly make her look friendly. I realized that I was probably staring and went back to my clothing search, as the mom and girl sat down on the seats beside the front door. I could hear paper being rustled and the busy scratching of a pen on a page. I heard the mom say in a whispered hiss, "I'm *not* happy about this."

"Well, I am," the girl replied quietly. "It's nearly the happiest day of my life."

I found one, but not both, of my sister's lost sweaters, and I was about to go back out to the playground to find Gina when Mrs. Reilly called to me. "Kieran Beck, just the person. This is Julia, and she'll be joining Miss McLennan's class. Can you take her outside and show her where her classroom is?"

The girl's good-bye to her mom was short and strange. "See you."

Her mom's arms were folded, and she had not once taken off her sunglasses. "Yes," she replied in a tight voice, before walking straight outside and down the path that led to the street.

"This way," I said to the new girl, shaking off my surprise at how things could be for other kids and their parents. "I'll show you where you can leave your bag. The bell won't go off until five to nine. I'm in Mr. Garcia's class. Your room is right next to ours —" I stopped then, thinking that I might sound too weirdly friendly.

We walked onto the playground before she spoke. "Kieran," she said. "So *you're* Kieran."

"Yes," I replied, shrugging it off, "that's me."

"Kieran," she repeated, more to herself than to me.

I let myself look at her properly. The new girl was tall and wore jeans, a checked shirt, and riding boots instead of a school uniform. Her blond hair was unusual, long in the front and cut into a short upward curve in the back. When she turned and I could see her pale-blue eyes clearly, it was as though she had traveled from somewhere foreign and quite different from our town and this school. Afterward, as we lined up for morning class, she seemed to be looking at each of us in turn. It was not in the worried way that some new kids did, but with a confidence I found fascinating and different. If she heard Mason and Lucas talking their usual silly stuff, she took no notice. It was the same with the girls in the lines close to mine. I could see them staring at the new girl and whispering comments to one another. Someone laughed loudly. I thought that Julia seemed to already know us all — the boys who could bully anyone who seemed the tiniest bit different, the girls whose friendships could turn mean and unpredictable, and the rest of us who filled the classrooms and playground.

I wondered how long it would take for the competition to start, where everyone wanted to be her new best friend.

But there was someone else new. They had also been put into Miss McLennan's class, so at morning assembly time two unfamiliar kids were standing just a little in front of our class. The comments, whispering, and laughter began again.

"Hey, there's another new girl."

"No, it's not; it's a boy."

"It's a girl, idiot. She's got a braid."

"Well, how come she's wearing a boy's top?"

I couldn't tell right away, either. The new kid stood beside Julia and stared straight ahead. I could see then that kids were inching away from this other new person, making faces and maybe saying the sorts of things Mason, Lucas, and the other boys in my class were saying.

"But she's got a braid."

"Like in the fairy tale. *Rapunzel.*"

"Hey, Rapunzel! Let down your hair."

"Let me kiss you."

"Hey, is it a girl or a boy?"

"A girl, stupid. Look at the hair."

"What about that jacket, though? Doesn't look very girly."

"Dare you to go and ask her if she's a girl."

"Dare you to go grab his nuts. We'll know if it's a boy, then!"

"Lucas, that's disgusting!"

I honestly still couldn't tell. This other new kid wore fleece track pants and a blue jacket with a motorcycle graphic on the back. They had mousy-blond hair, the same as mine, except theirs was bound into a long braid that trailed down toward the bottom edge of the jacket.

While the boys around me joked and talked, I found myself looking as intently at this second new kid as I had gazed at Julia. And suddenly, the kid with the braid seemed to know that I was staring, because *he* turned around very slowly and met my gaze.

It was Bon.

"It's a boy," I said to Mason, Lucas, and the others.

"How do you know?" Lucas asked.

Bon and I hadn't taken our eyes off each other. "He's got a boy's face." My voice was flat, but my head raced with questions and disbelief. What was he doing here? His hair was much longer, though his clothes still looked as faded and ratty as I remembered from ages before.

At that moment, Bon raised his hand as if to say hello to me, but I turned quickly away. I didn't want anyone to know that we knew each other, much less that we were related.

Mason and Lucas were hitting each other's shoulders and laughing. "Check out his hair!" Even though, three hours' drive from a beach, Mason had a mop of blond surfer curls. And even though Lucas was always fussy about how his hair was combed and flicked, always checking it whenever he walked past his reflection in classroom windows. I thought that was a bit much, but said nothing because I had tried for months to work my way into the middle of Lucas and Mason's circle of friends. Laughing at the same things and saying the right thing at the right time was important.

I was itching uncomfortably at the thought of sharing school with Bon. I wanted to know why he was here and, most importantly, when he was going away again.

Later that morning, as the bell rang for recess to finish, I found my chance. I could see Bon over near where kids were beginning to line up for class time. I could see him looking around a bit helplessly, as though he were trying to recognize some faces or figure out which group he needed to be with. I wasn't about to help him.

"I was looking for you," he said suddenly. "But I couldn't see you."

"How come you're here?" I demanded.

"I found Gina, and she remembered me," he added, ignoring my question.

"What are you doing at my school?"

"We came here."

After two years, I had forgotten what his voice sounded like. It was odd and precise, as though he weren't used to talking with other kids. I was already finding it annoying. "What do you mean?"

He blinked and looked a bit dazed. "We drove here. In my mom's car."

"Another surprise visit," I said. "Just like last time. Have you told anyone you're here? Nan? My parents?"

"My mom is visiting Nan this morning," Bon replied. "Telling her that we are here and that I'm going to stay." It was as though he weren't hearing the anger in my voice. "I'm going to be here at school with you."

My mouth dropped open at the word *stay,* before I quickly said, "Well, don't hang around me. And don't tell anyone we're cousins."

"But we *are* cousins."

I took a step toward him. "Not here we're not." Our noses were nearly touching, and I was close enough to smell Bon's faint scent of sweat and pee. At least this time he hadn't said that strange thing about us being brothers. "Do you still have the toys you stole from my room?" I asked. "Bet you don't. *Thief.*"

I realized a few kids had stopped to look at us, and I stepped back from him. As I walked away, I turned just once to glance back. Bon hadn't taken a step, and the look on his face was as though I'd given him a slap. I felt unhappy and guilty, knowing that I'd spoken to Bon in a way I never would to anyone else.

I'm going to stay. I'm going to be here at school with you.

Everything suddenly seemed out of balance. I wondered how I was going to manage having my strange cousin here at school, all the while pretending that we didn't know each other. I *knew* he would tell. I *knew* that I was going to be putting up with other kids making smart-aleck comments about the two of us being related.

The teachers had only just begun to emerge from the staff room to take us back to class. Whenever they were a bit late, the class lines got noisier and noisier, with kids talking and joking around, sometimes until the noise became deafening.

Beside me, Mason and Lucas began a mock fight. Mason pretended to pummel Lucas in the stomach. Lucas flung himself around with loud, comic groans, before getting Mason in a headlock. Mason yelled out, "Rapunzel! Rapunzel! Come and save me!" Kids laughed and began looking around for Bon.

"Rapunzel!" Lucas shouted. "Don't kiss Mason. He'll turn into a frog!"

Then Mrs. Gallagher's voice sounded through the playground microphone, and gradually all the noise faded. Lucas released Mason from the headlock and the two of them stood as though they'd been behaving beautifully the whole time.

I could see Bon standing a few rows ahead of me with the rest of the kids in Miss McLennan's class. He was easy to spot, with his braid and blue jacket, but so was Julia, because she and Bon were standing beside each other again.

As Mrs. Gallagher reminded everyone about waiting politely for their teachers, I could see Bon and Julia talking quietly — about what? Were they friends already?

I felt a pang of jealousy. There was something about Julia, something that I really liked about her difference from everyone else at school. *So you're Kieran.* When she had said that, it was as though she already knew me.

At that moment, she turned around, her eyes finding mine. I couldn't read her gaze or the expression her face held. She looked back to Bon and whispered something to him.

They were talking about me.

Of course they would visit us sooner or later, Bon and Aunt Renee.

In fact, I was counting the hours and minutes down from the moment Gina and I arrived home from school.

"I saw that boy," Gina announced. "That boy who's our cousin. He was at school."

"Bon," Mom replied. "I know. He's in town with his mother. Did he talk to you?" she asked Gina, and then looked at me. "Did you see Bon?"

"I saw him," I replied in a voice I hoped sounded uninterested.

Mom wanted more detail. "*And* . . . what did he have to say?"

"Not much. That he was here with his mom." I dropped my bag beside the doorway to the living room and started thinking about snacks.

"Is that all?" Mom asked.

"Bon has a braid," Gina interrupted. "It's longer than mine!"

"He said he was going to stay," I replied. "That he was going to school with me."

"Stay?" Gina interrupted again. "Stay with us?" She looked pleased at that thought.

"What did he mean, going to stay?" I asked.

"Kieran, I don't quite know. Not yet."

I thought of Nan talking about all the times she had left messages on my aunt's phone and had no reply, and the months of not knowing where my aunt and cousin were. I knew Nan worried about Bon.

"He said Aunt Renee was visiting Nan today," I said.

Mom nodded. "She did. And we're probably next."

Dad came home from work, tired and unimpressed. "So they're at the trailer park?" he said, leaning against the doorway as Mom assembled dinner ingredients on the kitchen island. He was still in his work clothes. "It's pretty grim down there, you know. Not much of a place for an eleven-year-old to call home."

Mom replied carefully. "I'm not sure that the trailer park is going to be a permanent arrangement."

I had positioned myself at the dining table, along with homework that I usually did in my own room.

Nearby, I could hear Gina singing along to her favorite music show.

"Nothing is a permanent arrangement as far as your sister goes, Megan. Is Renee taking her medication?"

The word sounded like an alarm in my head. "What medication?" I asked.

"Nothing for you to worry about," Mom answered quickly. Then she added, "To help Renee think straight. To help her look after Bon." She frowned a little. "Do you *really* need to be doing schoolwork out here in the kitchen?"

"Honey," Dad asked Mom quietly, "why is Renee back in town? What's she after?"

Mom closed her eyes and shook her head. "I don't quite know. Not yet."

"She needs something," Dad said. "Or she wants something."

Mom sighed. "Yes. And there's nothing I can do about it, except be patient and wait to see what happens."

"What happens," Dad mumbled. "What happens is that something *will* happen."

"I think it's Bon," Mom said. "I don't think Renee is coping all that well."

"Ah," Dad said. "I think I'm getting the picture."

* * *

It took until the weekend for my aunt to visit. Instead of the boyfriend and the big black pickup, there was a small, ratty hatchback parked at our front fence. It had out-of-state license plates, a clue to where Bon and my aunt had traveled from.

She had come alone. "Where's Bon?" Mom asked.

"He's back in the camper drawing pictures," Aunt Renee replied.

"He's by himself?" Mom asked, concerned.

My aunt did not reply.

I was relieved Bon wasn't in the house, that I wouldn't have to talk to him or be asked to find things to do together—and have to make sure he wasn't touching or stealing my things.

But having my aunt in the house felt a little strange—and uncomfortable as well. It started exactly as I remembered it from before, with my aunt smiling at me and saying hello in a way that had me wondering if she had forgotten my name. She fussed over Gina, cuddling her and talking to my sister as though she were three years old rather than six. Then she ignored us altogether and began to talk to Mom, who freaked out a little when Aunt Renee went to light a cigarette right there in the middle of the kitchen. Instead, Mom steered her out to our back deck, a mug of coffee in one hand and the cigarette nursed in the other. No longer the center of Aunt Renee's attention, Gina wandered down to her playhouse, which sat in a corner of our backyard.

Dad had hung around for a little while before announcing, "I'm off to the shed. I need to get that mower fixed." He headed for the steps, leaving Mom behind on the deck with her sister.

"Are you sure Bon is OK by himself?" Mom asked again. "I was hoping to see him. The kids were looking forward to him visiting again."

I wasn't. My mouth dropped open in surprise, but nobody seemed to notice. Or at least Mom pretended not to.

"He was told to behave and wait," my aunt replied.

Mom went to say something more, but then changed her mind.

My aunt talked and talked . . . and *talked*. There was something secretive about whatever she was saying, and she kept ashing her cigarette with quick taps against the edge of the ashtray on the table. Mom listened patiently and didn't seem to get much of a chance to say or ask my aunt much in return. My attention hovered between the morning sports show I'd turned the TV on to watch and the conversation on the back deck. From what I had overheard, it seemed that Aunt Renee had been through lots of man dramas, job dramas, and rented-house dramas. I heard my aunt call Nan *our mother*. For the first time, I heard her mention Bon's name.

Are you listening to me? I replayed that voice from Dad's birthday party and pictured the hand clenching Bon's face. Both bits of memory were tied together, as tight as a knot. I couldn't stop feeling uncomfortable about my aunt being here. I was used to Nan, Mom, Dad, and their friends, who asked us stuff about the things we liked, or who shared jokes with us and sometimes joined in our games. My aunt was a mixture of talkative light and unsettling shadow.

Suddenly, her voice was raised. "How did *you* get here?"

I heard Mom's soothing voice saying something I couldn't make out, before she called, "Kieran! Come here, please!"

Bon was at our back steps, silent and staring.

"I asked you a question," Aunt Renee said to him.

"I walked," he replied. "I remembered the house and the way to get here."

"Bon, it's lovely to see you again," Mom told him with a smile, before turning to her sister. "Renee, really, it's fine. He's very welcome. He and Kieran can do something together. Kieran?"

"I was going to help Dad," I said, my heart sinking.

Dad's shed was suddenly a quiet, welcome destination, though I wasn't sure what I was going to help Dad with exactly.

Mom shook her head firmly. "Renee and I are talking. You keep Bon company. Show him some computer games," she suggested in an oddly bright voice.

"Mom," I muttered a little desperately.

Then she added, "Or go outside and kick a ball around. Go for a bike ride. There're two bikes, after all, and a spare helmet he can wear."

I hesitated long enough for Mom to frown a silent reply, a do-it-or-else death stare.

If Aunt Renee smelled of cigarettes, I knew from the first morning on the playground that Bon still had the scent of sweat and pee I'd noticed two years before. Which gave me at least one excuse not to get too close to him if it could be managed.

Bon had not even said anything like hello. "I don't have a bike," he said to no one in particular. "I've never had a bike. Kids get those for Christmas." He wore a blank, dreamy expression.

"Kids who behave themselves get presents," Aunt Renee said to him, and though it sounded like an accusation, Bon did not reply.

"*Kieran,*" Mom said a little more urgently.

"We've got a computer," I said, telling him the

obvious in a flat voice. "And there're games and stuff."
Unwillingly, I led him inside in the direction of the
computer. *Why me?* I groaned to myself, thinking that
whenever a friend from school visited, there had been
easy, funny talk and always something to go and do.
At least a computer game could mean no conversation,
and that maybe I could escape, which I did after a few
minutes of showing Bon a few games and sites. I left
him sitting silently at the computer and ducked out the
front door and down the side driveway, so that Mom
wouldn't see that I had left Bon behind in the house.

"Another refugee," Dad remarked when I turned up
in his shed at the back end of the yard. He called his
shed the Guys' Room. It was where he kept his weight-
lifting and gym equipment, his workbench, and his
beer fridge. There were sports posters on the walls and
a calendar with a bikini girl holding a pair of shock
absorbers. Sometimes Dad would have friends visiting. Ant and Split Pin were my favorites. Ant worked
on his parents' sheep farm ten miles out of town,
where he was known as Anthony by his mom and dad.
Dad called him a human database of funny stories.
Split Pin was so tall he had to duck his head whenever he walked through a doorway, and he had once
been a state champion soccer player. I had seen his
real name, Sam Pinnock, in gold letters on the sports

record board that hung on the wall inside the front doors at school. If Ant and Split Pin were visiting, it gave me a good excuse to hang around, knowing that Dad's buddies would include me in their talk and jokes. I'd sit with them on folding chairs around the doorway of the Guys' Room, laughing along and joining in with their conversations.

Dad had the shed to himself this time, until I wandered in.

"So your aunt's still up there going on and on," he remarked. He had part of the lawn mower dismantled, and there were carburetor and gasket parts laid out on the workbench. "She was driving me crazy. Please don't tell your mother I said that about her sister."

"Bon's here," I said. "He walked."

"I know, I heard the fuss your aunt just made. Poor kid. So where is he now?"

"Playing on the computer," I replied.

"Hmm. Not interested in the great outdoors, then?"

"I guess not," I answered.

But soon after, we heard voices in the backyard. Bon had teamed up with Gina, and they were over at the bikes. Gina's bike was small and bright pink, with beads on the spokes that rattled around when she pedaled. I could see Bon sizing up the other bikes, the nearly new BMX that had been my Christmas present and the older bike that it had replaced. He glanced down to where I stood in the shed doorway watching, then chose the older bike.

Our house might have been old and a bit cramped, but our backyard was large enough to ride bikes around and have a bit of fun. There was a bump and a slight drop where I could get my bike airborne if I pedaled hard enough, and a patch of gravel in the far corner where I could do skids and slides. Gina managed the yard well for a six-year-old who had recently asked Dad to take the training wheels off her bike. She pushed the little pink bike into motion and then pedaled furiously across the grass toward the back fence, looking quickly back two or three times to see where Bon was.

"Come on," she shrieked at him. "I'm racing you!"

Bon didn't set off quite as fast. One foot slipped from the pedal, and his bike twitched from left to right. Each time he pushed off, the bike wobbled and he stared intently at the handlebars and the ground, not quite able to get himself balanced. I guessed that he didn't know much about cogs and gears, either. If I'd been close enough, I'm sure his knuckles would have shown white from him holding the grips so tightly. It took him a while to catch up with Gina, and it looked as though he had barely ridden a bike in his life. It was painful to watch.

"You OK over there?" Dad called to Bon.

"Nope!" I laughed. "He's going to crash." There was no reaction from Bon, save for one panicked glance.

"Doesn't look as though he's ever ridden a bike before," Dad said. Then he looked sideways at me. "I remember you being a bit wobbly on a bike, too, at first. He's giving it his best shot."

I pretended I hadn't heard. Of course I was wobbly the first time on a bike, but I reassured myself that I had been a little kid who never even needed training wheels. Dad went back to his workbench then and left me to watch the two bike riders—Gina racing and Bon wobbling.

Shortly after came his mom's voice. "Where are you? Time to go!" She hadn't said his name. Bon wheeled the bike back to its resting place under the carport.

Dad waved a relieved good-bye in the direction of Bon and his mom, then disappeared back inside the Guys' Room. I saw him roll his eyes and shake his head.

"Are you coming to play tomorrow, Bon?" Gina asked, trotting along behind him as they walked out to their car. She at least found him interesting.

Mom came to find me.

"Why are you down here?" she demanded.

Dad blinked and looked a little surprised. "Fixing the mower—why? What's happened?"

"Not *you*," she groaned. "Kieran. He was supposed to be in the house looking after Bon. Weren't you?" She eyed me sharply. "Go and play," she instructed. Then she stepped into the Guys' Room and pulled the door closed behind her.

I stayed nearby, eavesdropping.

"Well," came Mom's voice. "You won't believe what Renee's just asked."

"Try me," I heard Dad reply.

"It was about Bon. She wants to leave him here."

"What, for a little vacation?"

"More than that."

Their voices dropped to a low hum, apart from the one swearword I heard Dad use.

I found my bike and rode aimlessly around the backyard and around my sister. Gina chattered about Bon and how she thought it was nice to have him as a cousin. I tried to make sense of whatever it was my aunt had said, and I hoped that my mom's anxious face and voice did not mean what I started to imagine.

"What did Aunt Renee want? It sounded important," I asked later.

"It was," Mom replied patiently. "But for now it's just between us adults. It's not anything you need to be worrying about."

"But you were talking about Bon," I persisted. "It's something about him."

I had pushed just that bit too hard, and I got the lecture from Mom that I didn't want to hear—how Bon was my cousin, that I needed to be a lot nicer to him. And was I helping him settle in at his new school?

I went into my room to peel off my sneakers and socks. And there on the bed sat my missing white horse and armored knight. Gone for two years, they had reappeared to ride across the hills of my blanket and pillow. Something about the knight seemed different. His outstretched arms still carried his flag and sword, but the flag was now wrapped in a small sheet of folded paper. When I picked it off and opened the folds, there was a message in tiny, messy writing, and it took a little while to figure out what it said.

Bon had written, *We were borrowed and have been on many adventures. Now at last we are home.*

Of course I pretended not to be interested.

But whenever I saw her on the playground, I tried to walk near to where she was, or somehow make whatever game my friends and I were playing veer close to Julia and the friends she had made. I hoped there would be a reason or excuse for her to talk to me, and I tried to hear what she was talking about, so that after a while, the sound of her voice was in my head whenever I wanted it. What spoiled this every time was the fact that wherever she was, Bon was there, too. Julia's new friends seemed to have become his friends, all of them girls. Bon kept away from us boys.

I put a lot of thought into where Julia might live, and her jeans and riding boots told me—a farm. Julia had to be an out-of-town girl whose parents had bought one of the horse or alpaca properties that spread themselves across the green hills outside our town. Some of the kids at school were from farms; I had been to a couple of birthday parties at houses that I felt quietly envious of afterward: huge backyards, land big enough for trail bikes or horses, dams deep enough to swim in and wide enough for paddling canoes. This, I wanted to think, had to be the sort of house where Julia would live.

While just about every other kid on the playground wore a blue-and-red school uniform, Julia always wore jeans and those brown riding boots. I imagined that as well as having a big house on a beautiful farm, Julia was the sort of girl who might have her own horse, and that I would one day see her mom dropping her off at school in a luxury SUV that towed a horse trailer. But Julia's mom didn't seem to fit this picture at all. I had seen her walking Julia to the school gate each morning, and she was there every afternoon as well, meeting Julia and walking her away. There was no car that seemed to be theirs, and I never saw them having a conversation with each other. Julia's mom walked quickly and anxiously and kept checking that Julia was keeping up. Watching this, I couldn't quite imagine them going home to a beautiful farm.

At the southern edge of our town, near the stockyards and warehouses, was a small knot of streets and houses that I'd heard Dad nickname Dodge City. The houses were all boxy and scruffy, and some of the rough kids at school came from here. So did a couple of the wilder guys Dad played soccer with.

Two Saturdays after school had started back, I trailed along with Mom and Gina for a morning of going to garage sales. One was at a house in Dodge City. I felt uncomfortable being there. There was unlikely to be anything I wanted, and in a town as small as ours I would probably bump into at least one kid I knew from school. Mom was always on the lookout for old teapots and plates, Gina usually found a doll, a toy, or some clothing, and I always hoped for — but never found — old soccer collector cards, or better still, something with player autographs. This sale, as far as I was concerned, would have nothing I was interested in.

The people had spread a few old pieces of furniture, toys, a lawn mower, and a jumble of car parts across their front lawn. Against a tree rested a tangle of old bicycles. Everything looked shabby and sad. Then a little kid came out of the house in her pajamas and exclaimed, "Mom, here's someone from my school. It's Gina and her big brother." I realized then it was the Pearsons' house, and sure enough, when the big brother appeared at the door, it was Troy from my class. He said an awkward hello, then waited hopefully in case I wanted to buy one of his old toys. I wasn't going to, but spent a few moments looking anyway. Then I saw someone else's feet come and stand near to mine.

"Hi—" I began, running right out of voice when I looked up and saw who it was. I tried again. "Hi, Julia."

"Hi," she replied, not using my name.

"Kieran," I reminded her, feeling weirdly nervous.

"I know. I haven't forgotten — Kieran."

I glanced back at the street, thinking I would see the fancy European car or luxury SUV I'd imagined Julia might have arrived in. No sign. "Does your mom like garage sales, too?" There were other adults looking at the bargains as well, but none of them was Julia's mom.

She looked at me and frowned a little. "No, I walked here."

"Do you live around here?"

"No," she replied firmly. "Over there." And she pointed vaguely at the edge of town that led to the highway. I tried to follow her finger and figure out exactly where she meant, but all I could see was the truck stop and the trailer park. I wanted a more exact answer.

"You live over *there*?"

Julia ignored or didn't notice my amazement. "Well, I wouldn't call it living there. My mom and I are staying at the trailer park for now." She paused and added, "Same as your cousin."

I sighed. So she knew. "For now?" I asked. "Won't you be around for long?"

She tilted her head to one side. "Maybe. Maybe not."

"Where did you live before?"

"Another town a bit like this. Out in the sticks."

"But where?"

"I can't remember the name. Just the look of the streets and the color of the school uniform." She looked at me. "You ask a lot of questions, for a boy."

It sounded strange not to remember the name of a place where you had lived. But I had run out of questions, and it seemed she was through all the answers she wanted to give.

I glanced behind and saw Mom already holding a couple of things she was going to buy. I could tell they were things she didn't really want, that they were being bought because she felt sorry for the people selling stuff on their front lawn. I'd seen Mom do that before, had heard her say why afterward.

Julia had stepped away from me to look at magazines piled in a cardboard box. I started to follow her so she'd talk to me some more, but she was already striding over to the tangle of bikes against the tree. She noisily separated them. Behind three others and right against the tree was a purple bike I hadn't noticed.

"This looks OK," I heard her say, and she wheeled it away from the tangle. She lifted and spun the wheels, tested the brakes, tried sitting on it.

I followed her. "That's a boy's bike," I remarked.

"I don't care." She laughed. "I've always wanted a bike." She looked at me, and a challenge of some sort crossed her face, stayed set in her eyes. "And now I've got a bike. My mom is going to be *really* mad." Her face brightened then. She paused and read the price tag that was stuck to the frame. "But it's worth every cent." Julia rummaged in her pocket and pulled out some crumpled bills. "Now I can go wherever I want," she murmured.

"What do you mean?" I asked, but was ignored. I tried something else. "Do you like our school?"

It was a short reply. "The kids are OK."

"Nicer than the kids at your old school?"

"I don't know," she answered quietly. "I never actually went to school there." Her pale-blue eyes met mine. "Now you're asking too many questions." She stood close enough for me to catch a soft fragrance of soap or shampoo, close enough for me to see the patterns on her earrings. "You hang around with those boys who think they're too cool for school. What are their names? Mason and Lucas."

I raised my shoulders in a slow shrug. "Yeah . . . I guess."

"How come you don't hang around with Bon?" she asked. "He's your cousin, after all."

I shrugged uncomfortably, glancing across to where Mom was searching through boxes of odds and ends.

I was disappointed that the conversation had turned to Bon. *Because he's weird. Because he steals things,* I wanted to say.

"I thought you guys would be friends," Julia told me. She raised one eyebrow a little and waited for me to reply.

"You're already his friend," I said.

"But I'm not his cousin. And you live here. You'll always be here, even if I'm not."

"Kieran!" Mom called from nearby. "We've finished looking. How about you?"

"I'd better go," I said, a little relieved I'd been called.

"Bon told me about his cousin Kieran, so I knew about you before I'd even met you," Julia said.

"How?" I asked.

Julia ignored the question. "Bon needs someone who cares about him," she told me. "And that's *you.*"

I opened my mouth to ask what Julia meant, but she

looked at me as though I should already know. Mom and Gina were waiting at the roadside for me. "I have to go," I told her, sighing. "See you at school."

Suddenly, Julia's hand was gently grasping my arm. Her other hand held the seat of her new bike, and in a whisper she added, "You should buy something, too. Before you leave. I think these people really need the money."

She let go and watched as I rummaged in my pocket for coins. It was as though one of my parents had told me to do something, rather than a girl about my age. I chose a plastic robot that transformed into a truck and then back again, and gave Troy Pearson more of my precious spending money than I really wanted. By the time I'd paid, Julia was walking toward the gate with her purple bike. I realized then that it was actually an OK bike, and with a cleaning up it could even look pretty cool. But Julia already knew that, because she had paid her money and was launching herself onto the seat. She turned to me and raised her hand in a single wave — and smiled. Surprised, I waved back and watched her ride away down the street. She had *smiled* at me.

So — she didn't live on a farm with rich parents. There was no fancy car, or a pet horse in a paddock. A camper at the trailer park didn't seem right to me, somehow, but then neither had her mom when I'd first seen them at school. It was as though they didn't fit together the way my family did. I didn't know where Julia had come from, and how long she was going to stay. Somehow, she and Bon had met before they both started school on the same day. Then I realized they would easily have found each other at the trailer park.

Bon needs someone who cares about him. I didn't want to understand why she had said this.

I thought you guys would be friends. I didn't want to be told this. Talking with Julia hadn't quite gone the way I'd expected.

"That's a face I haven't seen before," Mom commented as we climbed into our car. "Is she new at school? Does she have a name?" Working at the only supermarket in town meant Mom got to know most of the faces from around town.

"Julia," I replied.

"Julia? Julia who?"

"I don't know," I said. "Julia Someone." But I was tumbling last names around in my head. *Barrie, Barlow . . . Barrett. Julia Barrett.*

Without looking, I could tell that Mom had found something humorous and was smiling at me. "Julia Someone," she repeated. "Hmm."

I tried to ignore her, staring out the window as we

left the streets of Dodge City and headed back into the main part of town. I thought of Julia's wave and that single last smile, and I wondered if she would have anything to say to me back on the playground at school.

I knew, though, that I wasn't about to start looking after Bon. And I sure wasn't going to be his friend.

6

Dad was leaving me behind again.

Once more he had chosen Guthrie Street, with the steepest hill, and I launched myself at the slope with all the energy I could muster. Dad stopped long enough to smile at me before jogging away toward the old train station, leaving me to catch my breath and then stumble after him. I was determined to keep up.

Finally, after jogging past the old bridge alone, I caught up, but only because Dad had paused to talk. Lenny and Danno, who worked for the town, were on their early-morning rounds and had stopped to empty the sidewalk trash bin outside the convenience store. I could hear their laughing voices above the utility truck's idling engine.

"Watch out, Tony, the young fella's catching up!" one of them said, laughing. They both wore official town hats and fluorescent safety vests, and I could never remember who was who.

"Time to get going, then," Dad replied, glancing back at me and making it sound like a cheerful family joke.

Lenny and Danno cheered me on as I jogged past, and I managed a wave and a grin that I hoped made it look as though I had buckets of energy left over. I was so close behind Dad now that I could smell his sweat and hear his puffs of breath. And then I spotted Bon.

Although the Tealeaf Café still had a CLOSED sign on its front door, Bon was inside and seated at one of the tables. A tall mug steamed gently on the table in front of him. He was reading something, a comic or a magazine, and lifted a slice of toast to his mouth. He didn't see me outside, although I'd come to a stop to look at him and try to size up what was happening. There was no sign of his mom.

"He's having breakfast," I mumbled. "The café's not even open yet."

Bon kept reading, taking slow bites of toast and then a sip from the mug. Though he sat at an angle away from the front window and the sidewalk, I could see that his silly braid was frizzed out from being slept on, and the clothes he was wearing were the same ones he'd worn to school yesterday. *How,* I wondered, *can Bon's mom afford café breakfasts for him, but not a new pair of sneakers without worn-out toes?*

Then Kelsie Graney, who worked at the café, walked over to the table beside Bon. I could see her asking him something and then his head shake an answer. Kelsie sat at the table alongside Bon. She didn't talk, but simply watched him as he read his comic and ate his toast. Her eyes found mine from across the road, and she raised a hand to me and waved hello, before walking to the front door and turning the sign over so that it read OPEN.

I jogged away before Bon looked up and saw me. At the end of the next block, Dad turned briefly and waved a *Come on!* hand to me. I found one last burst of energy and began to sprint the length of the shops until, at the corner of our street, I caught up with him.

It would have been easy to say, *Guess where I just saw Bon!*

Except I didn't.

In our kitchen, Dad was goofing around with Gina. "You don't want to be hugging me yet, princess," he told her as she danced and jumped around him in her pink pajamas. "You'll smell like an old soccer player."

"Yuck!" She laughed. "Then I'll hug you when you're nice and clean."

Mom held her nose and said, "This kitchen smells of sweat and old socks. You males need to go and shower."

"That's me first, then," Dad called back as he headed up the hallway to the bathroom.

I lay down on the kitchen floor with my arms and legs spread wide. The tiles and my damp shirt were cold against my back.

Mom stood above me and shook her head. "I presume you're starving by now. Have something to eat, then go and get yourself cleaned up and ready for school." She paused. "You don't have to put yourself through this every time your dad goes off jogging, you know."

"But I want to."

Guess where I just saw Bon! I looked up at Mom, but said nothing about my cousin's breakfast at the Tealeaf Café before it had even officially opened for the day. I wondered if Bon ate there every morning, and I wondered where his mom was. The idea of Bon sitting down to eat breakfast in a camper with her didn't seem to work, no matter how hard I tried to imagine it. Something about what I'd seen that morning didn't have the feel of OK about it. I ate my own breakfast slowly, our kitchen filled with the noise of Mom and Gina laughing and joking around together.

I watched them from across the table. It looked like an easy job being six years old and the cute little sister.

Sometimes, being the eleven-year-old big brother seemed a lot harder.

Nan called Gina a lovely surprise when she was born, though I didn't think of my sister in those terms when I was responsible for walking with her to and from school, or whenever I was teasing her to make her scream and yell. Pulling the heads off her Barbie dolls and sticking them onto my fingers like puppets had seemed like a good idea on at least two occasions. At first, Gina had loudly charged around the house after me, shouting and complaining. But once I started using silly voices and wiggling my fingers for each of the Barbie heads, she got a dose of the giggles instead. I could be good at making my sister laugh, but she was also good at following me around when I wasn't in the mood.

I wondered what it might be like to have a brother instead.

We're brothers, we are.

It was a voice I didn't want in my head.

And then Gina asked, "Is Bon coming to visit again today?"

"Not as far as I know," Mom told her. "You were a good girl to be out playing with him the other day."

Gina was dividing her attention between eating

toast and drawing something in her sketch pad. "I like Bon; he's nice."

"I agree," said Mom. "Don't you, Kieran?"

It was the last thing I wanted to talk about. "No," I mumbled.

Mom sighed. "You know, you and Gina have each other. Bon has only himself."

"*And* his mom," I pointed out. "He has her."

Mom shook her head. "I wouldn't say that, exactly. I think Bon has had to look after himself a great deal. A brother or sister could have been a good thing, or it could have made things more difficult than they are." Her face was serious, and she added softly, "She may be his mom, but she can't always give him the things he really needs. So there's something for you to think about. Especially when Bon is here, and when I ask you to spend time with him."

"But I don't *like* him. . . ." I muttered, feeling trapped in a stifling place where I was expected to be friendly with my only cousin.

"He's new in town and new at school," Mom said. "Imagine how you'd feel. It's important for Bon to make some friends."

"Well, he doesn't need me. He's got Julia Barrett. They're always hanging around together at school."

"Julia?"

"The girl who was at the garage sale. And Bon's already friends with *her*. He doesn't need me as well."

"School is different, Kieran. Bon is your cousin."

"He stole some of my things, don't forget."

"Kieran, he brought them back. Maybe you need to forgive him for that." She added, "I don't think Bon has much to call his own. We can only guess what he's left behind each time Renee has moved somewhere different. Or even *who* Bon has had to leave behind."

Without really wanting to, I found myself thinking of Bon saying good-bye to friends before he and his mom had gotten into their little car and driven all the way to our town. I wondered what sort of kids would put up with him. What I did know was that his silly hair and ratty clothes hadn't stopped him from being friends with Julia. *I* wanted to be friends with Julia.

"I don't like him," I said again, but my voice was a grim whisper to myself.

I was jealous.

When Dad took Mom out to dinner for their wedding anniversary, Gina and I had a Friday-night sleepover at our grandmother's.

Nan's house was very much Gina's and my territory;

it was where we visited every Tuesday and Wednesday after school, until Mom finished her afternoon shift at the supermarket on Sheridan Street. It was where we stayed if our parents wanted an evening out.

Except now I wasn't the only grandson in town.

I knew right away that Bon had been there, because an unfamiliar piece of artwork was stuck to the fridge in Nan's tiny kitchen, just beneath the magnetic frame with its photo of Bon, aged nine. In colored felt-tip pen, the picture showed an underwater scene with a shipwreck, schools of fish, and hammerhead sharks. There was enough detail to fill the entire sheet of paper. Bon had scrawled something at the top, which I couldn't be bothered to try reading.

"Bon did that," Nan remarked. "Good, isn't it?"

"It's *very* good," Gina agreed, which was about three more words than I would have offered.

"He stayed here Wednesday night," Nan said, taking ingredients from the fridge. Gina, her assistant cook, knelt on a stool and lined up the ingredients in a neat row on the counter. "The first time he's ever stayed," Nan said with a smile. Her smile dropped to a serious line and she added, "Actually, the first time he's ever been allowed to."

I scowled at the artwork on the fridge door before taking my overnight bag into the spare room where I slept whenever Gina and I stayed over. Nan kept a collection of old kids' things in the spare room—comics, jigsaw puzzles, toy cars, dolls, and books—that had belonged to my mom and perhaps Aunt Renee when they were young. Sometimes I found something interesting to look at and play with, but not nearly as often as Gina did. Nan's computer was off-limits to us both. "You spend far too much time on your own computer as it is," she had told me, and her backyard was too small and steep to kick a soccer ball or ride a bike around. Bon must have found the spare room interesting, because nearly everything had been pulled out and then put back differently and haphazardly.

Nan and Gina were cutting vegetables at the island in the center of the kitchen. I stood opposite and watched them a moment before asking, "How come he stayed here?" I knew I sounded grumpy.

"Because his mother—" Nan began, but stopped to think. Then, in a softer voice, she continued. "Because when Renee came to visit, she asked if he could. I couldn't say yes quickly enough. It's been difficult having them living so far away—in all sorts of places. Barely calling or visiting in all those years . . . so it was a wonderful chance to talk with Bon properly and get to know him better. I've really missed him all this time."

Of course, I knew that. I knew because of the photo, and I knew because of the cards and gifts Nan had tried to send on birthdays or at Christmas.

"Will he come and stay again?"

"Yes, he will." Nan stopped her cutting and murmured, almost to herself, "He will." She looked up at me. "Come here, Kieran."

When I did, she wrapped one arm around my shoulder. Her dangly earrings clunked against my head. "I don't know how much longer Renee is going to be in town, but Bon could be staying for quite a while. You need to know that."

"What do you mean? How long will he stay?"

Nan sighed. "I don't know just yet. Weeks, months. Maybe even longer."

"Yay!" Gina cheered. Without actually meaning to, I groaned out loud.

"Kieran, what is it?" Nan frowned.

"It's just that . . ." I sighed, thinking of what I had seen on the playground at school over the past two weeks — Bon staying close by Julia and the girls, or else sitting alone reading. Or drawing stuff in a book. I had been careful not to get too close to see exactly what he was drawing or writing.

"He's weird," I managed to say. "The way he looks and what he says and does. And it's weird having him at my school." I added defensively, "Other kids say stuff about him. It's embarrassing."

"Do you stand up for Bon when that happens?" Nan asked. "Do you actually speak to him at all, Kieran?"

I shrugged.

"*I* speak to Bon at school," Gina commented.

Nan sighed. "He's had a very different life than you've had. He's not weird, Kieran, just different. Different and weird are not the same." She unwrapped her hugging arm and returned to the dinner ingredients.

After a moment, I had to ask, "So what did Bon do while he was here?"

"Do?" Nan asked. "He drew that underwater picture, he read books, and he looked at the music files on my computer."

"*We're* not allowed on your computer," I said indignantly.

"You've got your own computer at home," Nan pointed out. "He doesn't. What else? We talked while I got dinner ready. We ate and then watched television. I made him wash that mop of hair and then dried and brushed it out for him. It took *ages,* let me tell you. But I had trouble getting him off to bed, because it seems he's not used to normal bedtimes." Nan raised an eyebrow. "Are you jealous, Kieran?"

"*No.*"

"I like Bon," Gina said. "He's nice." She looked at me and added, "Bon doesn't do teasing stuff."

"And I like Bon, too," Nan said firmly. "There's a lot about him to like. Or that needs to be liked. Isn't there, Kieran?"

Sometimes Nan and Mom managed to look and sound exactly the same. In an unconvinced voice, I answered, "I guess."

Nan told me, "If other kids are giving Bon a hard time at school, it's your job to stand up for him, and to let the teachers know what's happening. And I want to know about it, too."

I didn't wait to be asked if *other kids* included me as well. Leaving Nan and Gina to cut and cook things for dinner, I took myself back to the spare room. I wanted to clean up every last puzzle, toy, and book until it all looked the way it normally did whenever I came to stay over.

Gina's voice echoed from the kitchen. "When can Bon have a sleepover at *our* house?"

Mom shook the backpack as though she were weighing it. Then she undid the zipper and stared at the contents.

"Is this all you've brought?" she asked Bon.

"I just have the essentials," he told Mom in his odd, precise voice.

Then Gina dragged Bon away to watch TV with her in the living room. I didn't follow.

Mom set the backpack on the kitchen table and began emptying out the contents. She did it slowly, as though each item of clothing were going to tell her a story about Bon, and maybe about his mom. I mentally compared each item to my own things stowed neatly in my bedroom dresser, wrinkling my nose at faded colors, ragged threads, and holes. The worst thing I spotted was a wool hat. It had the sort of rainbow colors a preschool kid would wear, with an elf point at the top and five or six pom-poms hanging all around.

I snorted and laughed. "He wears *that*?"

Mom looked at me and shrugged. "If it's something he likes, it's quite OK." She put it over her hand and turned it around. "This isn't from a store; someone knit it. I wonder who."

"Aunt Renee?" I suggested, but Mom's eyes grew wide and disbelieving at that.

"This is sweet, actually," she said, almost in a whisper.

"*Sweet*," I repeated, muttering the word like a poison.

The last things from the backpack were a paperback novel from our school library and a sketchbook. I recognized it as the one I'd seen Bon hunched over at school.

Mom looked at the scrawled writing on its cover and read, *"Bon's Book of Maps and Inventions."* She flicked through a few of the pages and smiled.

"What's so good about that?" I asked.

"It's interesting," she answered. "And he's good at drawing. I never would have guessed."

"But his writing is disgusting," I commented, not curious at all about his silly drawing book.

Mom stopped at a page and then read, *"We traveled to a new and distant village, found lodgings, and began to observe the people and their ways."*

"He could have copied that from anywhere, Mom."

"Bon might have a good imagination and thought it up all by himself. What's the matter, Kieran?"

"Why does he have to sleep in my room?"

"Because it's important. He's our guest *and* he's your cousin. I'm not going to park him on the sofa or on the floor somewhere. He has to feel welcome." I frowned. Mom said in a stern voice, "I'm not going to argue with you about it, Kieran. Look—" She pointed at the clothing spread across the table. "These are what Bon calls his essentials. It's a little snapshot of his life— everything secondhand, close to worn-out, and not recently washed, either. Poor kid. Go and get some of your pajamas."

"Why?"

"To lend to Bon, because he's got none here of his own, and because I'm planning on throwing everything he does have into the wash tonight, including whatever he's wearing right now. We *have* to organize more clothes for him, something better to wear to school, something to get out and play in."

I chose my least favorite pajamas for Bon.

In a cartoon I had once seen, a kid had drawn a chalk line down the middle of his bedroom floor, which his sister wasn't allowed to cross. I felt like doing the very same thing, but knew I'd be in trouble for at least two different reasons. Unlike Gina, I hadn't had a friend stay over in a long while. I tried not to think too much about the last time, because it was someone who had moved away and I didn't see anymore.

So later, when Bon walked hesitantly into my room after a shower, dressed in the borrowed pajamas, I waved a pointed finger across to where the trundle bed had been set up beneath the window. "That's your side of the room," I said, hoping it sounded like an instruction to be obeyed.

Bon looked down at the trundle bed, which sat on an empty rectangle of carpet. "OK," he said quietly, but I saw him glancing across at the medieval castle, and I knew he was longing to touch and play with it.

"Don't even *think* about touching anything that's not yours," I added.

Bon didn't argue back. He looked away and started rustling inside his backpack, which was empty of everything now, except for the silly drawing book and the even sillier wool hat. It was the drawing book and a black pen Bon pulled out. He turned away from me then and stretched out along the trundle bed, with the open book cradled away from my sight.

I looked across at my castle. I hardly ever touched it anymore, though sometimes I'd rearrange the figures to make things just a bit different.

"Have you grown out of it?" Mom had asked once or twice. "Do you think it's time to pass it on to someone else?"

But I couldn't. The castle and its figures had been special birthday gifts, and they reminded me of a friend I still missed.

The no-Bon side of the room still felt uncomfortably close to the Bon side. And while the no-Bon side had all the things I owned and liked, somehow the Bon side seemed to creep across the floorboards, ready to take over my whole room. I clicked on the reading light above my pillow and tried to concentrate on one of Dad's sports magazines.

There would have been complete silence in my bedroom, except for the frantic scratching of Bon's pen as he worked in his book. I put up with the noise for as long as I could stand it, which was about three minutes.

"What's all that stuff you're drawing?" I grumbled, keeping my face buried inside the magazine.

"A map," he said, his voice a little muffled. I guessed that he wasn't looking at me, either. "I like drawing maps of imaginary places. And I draw dragons and castles, and write clues for where to find treasures—" He stopped abruptly. For a moment, he had sounded bright and almost cheerful, but must have remembered it was me he was talking to.

I lowered my magazine. "How can you even read what you've written? Your writing's disgusting."

Bon didn't look up. "Miss McLennan says my brain works faster than my hand."

"Does Miss McLennan ever mistake you for one of the girls?"

I could see his eyebrows creasing into a frown. I knew I was being mean, but couldn't stop myself.

"Because of your hair," I said. "That stupid braid."

"This is how much my hair has grown in four years," he answered, as though making an announcement. "Native American braves used to wear their hair long because it showed that they were strong."

"Strong? Is that why you're doing it? I've never seen you play any sort of game at school, and I've seen you trying to ride a bike here at home. I could beat you at *anything.*"

Bon was silent for a moment. "Not at drawing maps of imaginary places. Or knights on horseback," he said, his pen scratching on the page. "Or at drawing inventions."

"Inventions?" I laughed back. "You're weird."

"I've got an invention for solar-powered interactive

television, and a mousetrap that doesn't kill the mouse," he said.

I snorted in disbelief. "You are weird. Anyway, someone's already come up with that kind of mousetrap and most likely the television as well. Solar power's been around for ages."

"Not *my* kind of mousetrap or television," Bon answered, keeping his eyes on his pen and his page.

Curiosity got the better of me, and I sprang off the bed to steal a look at whatever Bon was drawing. I had enough time to see two figures in armor riding two horses. Each rider had their helmet off and their hair blowing behind them, and I was surprised at how realistic the picture looked. It wasn't only underwater scenes, like the one on Nan's fridge; Bon could really draw. I had to admit that. Above the picture was a scrawled sentence, and in the moment before Bon slapped the pages shut, I managed to read *Bon the Crusader* and *Julia the Fair*.

"How come you're always hanging around Julia?" I demanded. "It must drive her nuts having you following her everywhere."

Bon looked up at me again, but took a long moment to actually say anything. "Because we're friends," he answered at last.

"Friends? I think she just feels sorry for you."

"Well, we *are* friends. We like the same things, and we talk about the same things."

"Like what?"

"Like . . . *things*. About ourselves and what we're thinking."

I wanted to say more. I wanted to turn *Bon the Crusader* into a clever insult, but *Julia the Fair* would be caught up with the insult as well. I looked over at my medieval castle and its army of figures, realizing that Bon had stolen my toys two years before to draw them, and that he must have practiced lots and lots in the time before he had brought them back.

We are friends. We like the same things, and we talk about the same things. Jealousy flooded over me. Julia hadn't talked to me since the morning at the garage sale. I wondered what it would be like having her here at my house, instead of Bon, and wondered what we would talk about. There was nothing I could think of talking about with Bon.

I would much rather have had Mason or Lucas here for a sleepover, but they always seemed to be busy with something else whenever I'd asked. Instead, I had a cousin I barely knew or liked here in my room.

"Huh," I mumbled behind my magazine. If Bon had heard me, he didn't let on, and for once, it felt like forever until Mom came to the doorway.

"Sleep time, lights out," she said, coming over and giving me the usual good-night kiss. I flinched and hoped that Bon wasn't watching, but he was — in fact, he was staring, as though a good-night kiss were something he'd never seen before. And then Mom was over with him, kneeling down beside the trundle bed. "Good night, Bon. There's a flashlight under your pillow if you need to get up in the night. Will you be OK?"

She leaned over and gave him a kiss as well. It felt strange to see that happen, and Bon looked so surprised at first. Then his face softened into something that was almost a smile.

In the darkness afterward, I could hear him murmuring to himself. It was as though he were having a conversation with someone.

"Shut up," I said at last. "Go to sleep."

There was a moment more of his whispering. "Good night, Kieran," he said softly, and then was quiet.

I didn't reply.

In the morning as we got ready for school, I looked at Bon with quick, sneaky glances, because there were things I was suddenly curious about. He peeled his pajamas off in an absentminded kind of way and then slowly assembled the things he needed for school. I glanced sideways and cautiously, almost expecting him to look different in some strange and surprising way—that maybe he had a sprawling birthmark, a terrible scar, or no belly button, or that he wasn't actually a boy at all. But in truth, he was just like me: skinny and pale, the same height, and with all the same details. I felt embarrassed then for looking, and I said to him gruffly, "Get dressed, or you'll make us late for school."

Mom had three packed lunch boxes lined up on the kitchen island.

"Is this mine?" Bon asked when Mom handed him the third one.

"Of course it is. I wouldn't be letting you starve, Bon. Hasn't Nan given you a school lunch when you've stayed with her?"

"Yes, but . . ." He turned the box over. "It's got my name on it." He sounded a little amazed.

"Because I wrote it," Mom answered. "It's yours to keep."

I shook my head, remembering Gina getting excited over having her own lunch box and drink bottle when she'd started kindergarten. Someone Bon's age getting excited about a lunch box seemed really strange. "Haven't you ever owned a lunch box before?" I snorted.

Mom frowned at me. I'd expected that, but not Bon's answer. "No," he said.

When it came time to start out for school, Bon made one more trip to get his backpack from my bedroom, and I almost followed him to make sure he didn't touch or take something. He reappeared, wearing the wool hat with the pom-poms.

"You're not wearing *that* to school!" I exclaimed.

"It's cold," he replied. "It's my favorite hat and it keeps my head warm."

"I like it," Gina remarked.

"You would, because it's for little kids," I said.

Gina told Bon, "Kieran has a ski hat with flames on it. When he puts it on, it looks like his head is burning." She giggled, and I got annoyed because I thought I saw Bon smile. Then Gina pleaded, "Can I have a turn wearing your hat tomorrow? *Please,* Bon?"

I felt horrified at the thought of being seen with someone wearing such a weird thing on their head. The tallest pom-pom stuck high above Bon's forehead, and the longest drooped down almost to his shoulders. It made him look like an elf, or, worse, kind of a baby.

"Can I ride my bike to school?" I asked Mom desperately.

She shook her head. "You'll walk with Gina, just as usual."

"Bon can walk with her; he's here today."

"What's wrong with the three of you walking together? When Gina's old enough, she can ride her bike to school and then so can you."

I didn't want to be seen arriving at school with Bon and his silly hat, and I could imagine now what would happen — kids laughing, hands grabbing, and the hat being thrown from hand to teasing hand, until it wound up on the ground or on a classroom roof. And Bon would be reaching out uselessly, saying, "Give me back my hat, please," in his precise voice.

So we stayed together for as long as I knew Mom would be watching from the front gate, but as we walked around the corner onto Hanley Street, I let myself fall behind Gina and Bon. I could have worked up a good speed if I'd been able to ride my bike. I would have beaten them to school and been well away on the playground with my own friends. Instead, I was stuck with both of them, my little sister and my strange cousin. I trudged along behind as though my sneakers had soles of concrete.

CHAPTER

8

Bon's wool hat did not wind up on a classroom roof. But it did get pulled from his head and passed around like a football, until eventually someone threw too hard and the hat dropped to the ground. Mason, Lucas, and the rest of us took turns stamping our feet on it, as though we were killing a venomous spider. When that became boring, we walked away. Even with fierce Mrs. Barnes on playground duty not too far away, we had made it all look like a game. I had expected Bon to make a fuss or to cry even, but he danced awkwardly around the outside of our circle as his hat was thrown from hand to hand. He had not said a word. Focused on the fun, I avoided looking at his face, but I felt guilty and wondered if he would say anything to Nan or Mom.

"Uh-oh," Mason said. "Here comes Gay Boy's friend." And we walked away together, avoiding Julia's approach. When I looked back, she was on a playground seat beside Bon. She dusted off his wool hat and gave it back to him to put on again. I turned away quickly so that our eyes would not meet, and I laughed at Mason's comments about weird new kids at our school.

I often spotted Bon on the playground sitting with her, or walking around and talking with her. I saw how he tagged along behind the friends she had made, but always seemed to be outside the conversation circle, until Julia made sure he was included. Sometimes, he'd give up and go sit down somewhere with his book of maps and inventions. I wondered if Bon actually knew how to make friends.

Julia did. She was like a magnet to the other kids in her class and had quickly stopped being the new girl. People wanted to be her friend. I heard her talking about this school as though it were an interesting project she had taken on. *Why doesn't your school do this?* Or, *Why doesn't your school have this?* Julia had plans and schemes for games, activities, and the way the playground was set up, and the ideas she came up with became some of the things we talked about in class. *The little kids have jungle gyms, but what about the big kids? Can we do horseback riding for a school sport? Can we camp out in tents on the playground one night? Can we go on a field trip to the beach?*

But I knew that Julia hadn't been to school wherever

she had lived before, even though she seemed to know a lot about other schools and other places. She hadn't meant to tell me that, and I hadn't mentioned it to anyone else. I wondered if she had ever been to school *anywhere*. There was a mystery about Julia that I quite liked, but it bothered me, too. I wondered how much she had told Bon.

Away from Julia, Bon said not much at all. Boys would call out *Rapunzel* or *Hey, Gay Boy;* they would sometimes bump into him on purpose or put a foot out to try to trip him. I did the same things as well, and then would ignore his blank, unblinking eyes when he stared at me. I tried not to think of it as an accusing look. But Julia always seemed to know.

One day we found Bon sitting alone on the seat outside the library, and Mason gave Bon's braid enough of a tug to make Bon cry out. When Bon stood up and tried to walk away, Lucas put a foot out to make Bon stumble. Knowing Mason was watching, I did the same thing. Bon said nothing. He simply stared at us and tried to keep walking. It was all set to happen again, until Mason said, "Uh-oh, here she comes again, Rapunzel's friend." He made it sound like an insult.

From wherever Julia had been on the playground, she had seen what was happening and strode across.

"You guys are being bullies," she said, standing

face-to-face with Mason and Lucas. "This school has a bullying problem and you are it."

This was greeted by *oooooh*s as Julia's statement was laughed away by Mason, Lucas, and the other boys from my class. I tried to melt into the back of the group and not be seen or heard.

"And this school," replied Lucas, "has a busybody issue." He pointed a finger at Julia and smirked. "And you, Julia Barrett, are it." There was a chorus of cheers.

Julia stood her ground. "Pathetic. All of you. You think you're cool, but you're not. Ganging up like idiots. You're the dumbest boys I've ever known."

"Like we care what you think." Mason laughed. "You don't run the school."

"You don't run the playground. Leave Bon alone. He's got as much right to be here as you, or anybody," Julia replied.

"Yes, *Mom*," Lucas sneered. "Anything you say, *Mom*."

Then came the one thing I didn't want to happen.

"Kieran," Julia said. It was a pointed, scolding voice. "Bon is your cousin. You should be looking out for him, not just copying what these losers are doing."

I began to walk away. She followed.

"It's mean, Kieran. Are you that mean to anyone else?"

I stopped abruptly and faced her, wanting to ignore

those pale-blue eyes, but knowing I couldn't. "No," I admitted.

"I didn't think so," Julia said quietly.

She turned away then. I looked down at her riding boots, watched them stepping away and standing beside Bon's sneakers, bought new by Nan. Bon's eyes found mine before he walked away with Julia.

She had just done exactly what I'd seen her do ever since the day she came to our school: be both defender and peacemaker. She was behaving as though she were Bon's older sister, or even — I realized, blinking with surprise — as though she were his mother. That thought was interrupted by my group walking over to me.

"Hey, Kieran," Mason was the first to say in his loud, listen-to-me-everybody voice. "Rapunzel's cousin, huh? How lucky are *you*!"

"That's old news," I muttered.

"Hold his hand, Kieran."

"Make sure he wears his pretty hat in the cold weather."

"Make sure he remembers his manners. Please and thank you."

"Give him a kiss to make him feel better."

"And a hug. He likes a hug."

I didn't answer any of these comments, because my stomach was suddenly full of butterflies. Julia had told me another uncomfortable truth, and I wished she had said something completely different. I wished that I could be somewhere else.

The bell rang for the end of recess.

Mason used a silly girly voice to repeat one of his dumb comments, so I gave him a shove, hard enough to make him stumble backward.

"What was that for?" he said loudly. "You can't take a joke all of a sudden?"

On the way to class lines, nobody spoke to me. Trying to shrug off what had happened, I joked around a bit with Lucas and Mason. "He might be my cousin, but he's still a loser," I told them. Lucas agreed, although Mason was still in the process of forgiving me for shoving him.

I felt caught up in the group that gave Bon a hard time, tripping him or calling him names away from where teachers could see or hear. Whenever Lucas and Mason and the others decided it was time to bother Bon for fun, I hovered at the very edges of the teasing, keeping my hands and feet to myself, staying silent and hoping that my friends wouldn't notice the difference. I wanted to imagine myself invisible and so went on ignoring Bon at school as much as possible, saying nothing whenever I saw him being chosen last for a team during gym, and pretending not to hear him when he said, "Hi, Kieran." Which was every single morning when our paths happened to cross on the playground or on the way to class.

I heard from Mom that Bon and Aunt Renee had left the trailer park and now had a hotel room in the center of town. How much better that was I couldn't be sure, but there had been little differences I noticed about Bon over only a few weeks — the new sneakers, matching school clothes, and a winter jacket, all replacing the frayed, faded clothes he had first arrived in. I knew that Nan and Mom were the ones giving Bon all these things, all this attention. In the meantime, I went to birthday parties he wasn't invited to and was part of playground games he would always be left out of.

But I couldn't ignore the fact that Julia was his friend and protector. He went on hanging around her friends and their conversations. She walked him around the playground, the two of them nodding, talking, and, I guessed, sharing secrets. At the end of some lunch breaks, I'd see them coming out of the school library, along with the other kids who liked books or chess.

"Hi, Julia," I'd say whenever we passed each other on the way to class lines, or were waiting near each other in the cafeteria to buy snacks. It was always an effort to say anything else to her, and I found myself hoping she would say something more in return.

But she'd always reply, "Hi, Kieran," and give me a look I read as, *I've seen how you and your friends treat Bon. You're still not looking out for him, are you?*

And at the end of some school days, I'd often see Julia and Bon stopped somewhere short of the school gates, sitting on the grass near the school office. If they weren't talking, they'd simply be sitting and watching everyone else walk by. Now that Julia often rode her bike to school, I didn't see her mom at the school gate anymore. So Bon and Julia taking their time was as though they were putting off their journeys home, to a trailer park and a hotel room.

"We should wait for Bon," Gina would sometimes say at the gate. "He can walk with us some of the way home."

I would shake my head. I didn't want Bon to get the idea that he was welcome to walk to or from school with us anytime he liked. Having him with us for some of the time already was more than enough. So I chose different ways to get home, along the other streets that would lead us to our own. I tried to ignore Gina's complaints about the extra hill to walk up and the scarier dogs that lived at several houses along the way. Bon could find his own way to his own home.

"I can see Bon over there," Gina said.

"He's with his friend Julia," I told her. "He'll be a while yet. Come on, let's go."

"But I want him to walk with us," she insisted.

"No, Gina. Come *on*," I urged, watching as Julia took off on her purple bike.

Gina sighed, disappointed. "All right."

I hurried her along a bit so that Bon wouldn't spot us and want to catch up. I led Gina the longer way, down the hilly sidewalks to the Sheridan Street shops.

"I want a snack," Gina announced as we came to the supermarket. "Chips or gummy worms? I can't decide."

"Only if you share," I told her. "And it's not one of Mom's workdays, so you'll have to spend your own money."

Gina dropped her school backpack on the sidewalk and triumphantly pulled out a coin purse. "I've got spending money." She grinned.

"Aisle six," I reminded her as we walked inside.

"Chips or gummy worms?" she repeated to herself as she disappeared into the aisle. "I still can't decide."

For Gina, these decisions were never quick, so I had time to wander around a little. I stopped to look at the magazine racks.

Then I heard the voices.

"You are not getting your photo taken," said a hushed, annoyed voice that I recognized.

"I *am*." This time it was Julia's voice, not quite as hushed. "I haven't had a school photo for two years. You can't stop me."

They were in the aisle right next to where I stood, and I peered along the gaps in the shelves until I could catch a glimpse of them. I couldn't see their faces, but I could see the top Julia had worn to school that day, and I recognized the silver bangle on one wrist.

Her mom wore jeans and a black jacket. "I'll keep you at home," she said in an urgent voice.

"Huh! Home — a filthy camper!"

"I've told you the rules before. You shouldn't —"

"I'm going to school that day and every day."

"You shouldn't even be there. I was stupid to listen to your complaining." And her mom added, in a voice like a little kid's, "'Oh, I'm lonely. I've got no one to play with.'"

It felt strange and unexpected to be hearing all this. From aisle six, Gina said loudly, "I'm choosing gummy worms, because the red ones are still my favorite."

And at that very moment, I heard Julia say, "I shouldn't even be with you!"

I found Gina at the checkout, and I helped her with the coins for her gummy worms. "Wait for me out-side," I told her, and she walked out to where we'd left our schoolbags beside the supermarket doorway.

I hovered a moment more at the checkout before Julia appeared from a nearby aisle. She was empty-handed, pale with anger, and looked surprised and embarrassed to see me there.

"Hi," she managed to say. It wasn't the confident voice I was used to hearing.

"Hi, Julia," I said awkwardly. Behind her was her mom, who was no taller than I was. Her eyes were still hidden behind dark glasses. She held a small basket of groceries, and I probably stared at her a bit longer than was polite.

"Who are you?" she demanded.

"Kieran," I replied quickly, feeling as though I was in trouble for something. "And that's my sister, Gina," I added, pointing to the doorway.

"They're Bon's cousins," Julia said.

"*Oh.*" It was a reply loaded with recognition. "Nice to meet you." But her voice was flat and unconvincing.

"I have to go," I said, knowing how nervous my own voice suddenly sounded. "See you tomorrow, Julia."

"Yeah, see you. At *school.*" The last word came out with emphasis, and Julia said it to her mom rather than to me.

It was a relief to get outside again. I was glad it wasn't one of Mom's shifts that afternoon. I could still feel Julia's mom glaring as Gina handed me a gummy worm and we set off for home. Whether the glare was meant for me or for Julia, I couldn't be sure.

I shouldn't even be with you.

I wondered why Julia had said that.

The following week, we had our annual class photographs taken. The photographers set up bleachers in the back playground, and, class by class, we lined up and watched the groups ahead of us get organized and pose. I knew that the photographer would have every group of kids saying something like *Vacation!* or *Candy!* so that everyone would be smiling as the camera clicked. The class ahead of mine was Miss McLennan's, and I spotted Bon in the second row with some other boys. He was wearing his clean, new school clothes. His hair was brushed and neatly parted, and his braid was hidden from view, except for whoever had to stand behind him.

As the photographer started giving last-minute instructions about feet together and facing this way, I suddenly realized Julia wasn't anywhere to be seen. I looked carefully along each row of kids in Miss McLennan's class, but couldn't see her. Until I turned and looked behind. Julia was by herself on one of the playground seats beneath the shade trees, watching her class being photographed. Somehow she sensed I was watching her, and she met my concerned frown with a shrug that could have meant, *I'm OK. Everything is fine.*

Julia was not being photographed.

Miss McLennan called out to her.

"I'm not wearing the right clothes," Julia called back, and at first refused Miss McLennan's encouragement to join in.

"Everybody wants you here, Julia," she said. "You're very much a part of this class. Come on."

I saw Julia shake her head again, uncomfortably remembering the argument she'd had with her mom in the supermarket. It had been about this, the school photo. About Julia staying away from the camera.

And then, just as the camera began clicking, Julia stood up and strode over.

"I'm in!" she announced, and some of the girls cheered. She wriggled her way to a standing position in the middle row and her face lit up. I *really* liked that smile. Below her in the second row, Bon smiled as well. The two of them looked pleased and content, as though there had been no bullying on the playground, no arguments in the supermarket. I saw their happy faces and swallowed — hard.

When it came to our turn, I made sure I got into the back row, along with Mason, Lucas, and the cool kids. I figured that somebody was bound to make a face for the camera, or make rabbit ears with their fingers behind someone's head. It was another of those moments where I told myself it was easier hoping to be friends with Mason and Lucas, and all the other kids I'd ever known. Staying friends with them meant not being left out of things.

It seemed to take forever for the photographer to get our class just right, to have everybody standing just so. I watched as Miss McLennan gathered her class together and led them to the library for the individual portrait shots. Of course, Julia and Bon walked away together, and I could see them smiling and talking to each other. I wondered all over again about Julia's mom disliking the idea of school photos so much, and about Julia changing her own mind when it had nearly been too late.

I couldn't get Bon's happy face out of my head.

He's going to be here for a long time, Nan had said.

Then I thought about Gina and how I'd sometimes see her run up to him on the playground and take his hand, smiling and talking to him in a way she never seemed to do much anymore with me.

"When can Bon come to our house for another sleepover?" she had asked Mom more than once.

But the next time would be a lot more than a sleepover.

"Kieran's got his flame hat on," Gina said. "His head is on fire! Help, help!" She and her friend Emily fell into helpless giggles.

"Ha-ha," I replied in a bored voice. "It was only funny the first time, Gina. This is about the twenty-third time I've heard you say it." And I turned my attention back to soccer practice.

I had been asked to look out for Gina, and also for Bon, while Mom and Nan had dinner out with Aunt Renee. It seemed like a strange way for Mom and Nan to spend a Thursday evening, and I wasn't happy at all about Bon arriving at the soccer field, the taillights of his mom's hatchback bumping away onto the road that led back to the center of town. She had not even gotten out to walk Bon over and say hello; he found his own way to where we were all gathered to watch my dad and his team prepare for the weekend game. Bon looked a bit lost and unsure of where he was, but for a while, Gina and Emily took charge of him with their talk and laughter. And I was left alone.

The sun had fallen behind the western hills, and the playing-field floodlights flickered on. Even with the warmth of my wool cap and winter jacket, I could feel the night chill beginning to rise from the damp ground.

Dad and his teammates ran and dodged in patterns around one another. They stepped quickly to the left and right, before breaking into sprints from the half-way line to the goal zone. They called instructions to one another as each part of the practice unfolded. We watched from the sidelines: kids, wives, and girl-friends in talkative groups, little clouds of breath from us beginning to show as the air turned cold and the evening darkened.

I kept most of my attention on Dad, but also watched Ant and Split Pin, Terry, Ray, Jacko, and all the other guys I knew. I watched their moves and tech-niques, especially when the soccer ball was kicked onto the field and they played quick, five-a-side practice games. I wanted some of the skills to drift across in my direction. I wanted to be a talented player, too.

Bon had watched Dad and the team for a little while, but then wandered away with Gina and Emily to the kids' play area near the changing room, where he now sat on one of the swings. It moved very slightly to and fro.

There were some other kids from school, boys and girls, who had turned up with their dads. As usual, we waited impatiently to be called onto the field to join in a bit of a game with the team.

At last, one of the guys called out, "Come on, you kids! Get over here, pick a team, and show us old fellas how to play."

I peeled off my winter jacket and ran across the damp grass, joining the side that Dad was on. Kickoff was the signal for grown-ups and kids to chase the ball in puffing, crazy groups across the field. The wives and girlfriends called out from the sidelines, and there were jokes and laughter from the players as we fought for control of the ball and the crucial passes and kicks that might lead to a goal.

Someone—I wasn't sure who—kicked the ball completely wide of the opposing goal, so that it skated and bounced off the field and across to where Bon sat on the swing. He got a bit of a fright as it breezed past him, but stood up and retrieved it. Everyone on the field was calling to him.

"Kick it back here, kiddo!"

"Don't kick it to him; he's ugly! Send it over here!"

"Come on, give it a whack!"

Bon wasn't quite sure what to do. He trotted over toward the sideline, clutching the ball to his chest, while everyone shouted to him to send it their way. Then Dad jogged across toward him. "Here, Bon," he called. "Throw it this way."

Which Bon did, before retreating to the play area once more.

"Who's the girly-boy?" I heard one of the guys ask Dad. "I've seen him — or her — around town."

"Him?" Dad replied as he jogged back into the thick of the game. "That's Bon — he's my nephew. A good kid."

Girly-boy. I smiled at that. It suited Bon, I thought. *A good kid.* My smile dropped.

Dad's friend Split Pin was on our team, and at one point, he neatly hooked the ball and found a gap through to run with it. Finding myself parallel and within kicking distance of the goal net, I called, "Sam! Pass!"

I didn't know why I'd called him by his real name. Those gold letters on the sports record board at school, maybe. At any rate, I had my goal kick foiled by Jackson Anderson.

"Jacko's a great goalie," Dad told me afterward. "You did well to get that close."

After practice, when everyone was drinking thirstily from water bottles and putting jackets and sweatshirts on, ready for home, Bon came over and said, "Sam. Which one is Sam?"

I looked at him. His face was set and serious.

"How come you need to know?" I asked him.

"I just need to. I heard you call out to him when I was over there." He pointed back at the play area, then repeated, "Which one is Sam?"

"The really tall guy putting on the black jacket. What, you know him?"

Bon looked over at where Split Pin stood. "That's Sam?"

"Yes."

"Oh."

"You don't know him, do you?"

"No." Bon sighed. "I don't know him. He's a different Sam."

Bon was very quiet for the rest of the evening, enough for Dad to ask in the car on the way home, "Are you all right there, buddy?"

"I'm tired" was Bon's only reply, but I heard him in the darkness of our car, murmuring to himself. I stared at him as though he were a crazy person, and he abruptly stopped.

His mom was waiting for him in her car. It was

parked right outside our house, and Mom stood by the driver's window talking with my aunt for the minutes it took for Dad, Gina, and me to unload ourselves out of our own car and get inside, away from the evening chill.

"Bon didn't come and have a kick with us," Dad remarked afterward. "What does he do at school when it's recess?"

"He hangs around with the girls," I said.

Dad was more than surprised. "Really?"

"His best friend is a girl," I added.

Dad nodded his head. "Well, everybody's different, I guess," he said, dropping his gym bag in the hallway and heading for a shower. "Poor kid. He looked completely lost with that soccer ball tonight."

I heard the noise of my aunt's car leaving and our front door clicking shut.

"How was practice?" Mom asked.

"Good," Dad replied. "Kieran nearly got the ball into the net past Jacko Anderson. How was your dinner?"

Mom thought a moment. "*Interesting.* We worked through some issues. Made some important decisions." She glanced at Gina and me. "I'll tell you more later." Which I knew meant after my bedtime.

* * *

We saw Bon again early the next morning.

"Now, that's interesting," Dad said, stopping on the sidewalk across from the Tealeaf Café. Usually, he kept his eyes on the sidewalk or on the road ahead. He would jog the length of the Sheridan Street shops without stopping, and he would keep a sharp focus on every breath and step. He would only glance up when someone else walked nearby or he came to a curb and had to look for traffic. Dad might pause to say *Hi, guys* to Lenny or Danno as they emptied the bins, but would usually not stop until we came to Apex Park, where he would do his leg stretches, sit-ups, or simply lie on the grass for a few minutes. This was when we would talk—about the weather, the familiar people or cars we'd noticed while jogging, our guesswork about the warm scents that drifted from the bakery. Or we might talk about the approaching weekend game, about players and tactics.

But today was different. Dad had happened to glance across at the café as we passed by, and then he stopped in his tracks. Of course, I knew what he had seen. *Who* he had seen.

"It's Bon," he said between breaths. "What's he doing there? Kelsie's giving him breakfast, by the looks of things. So where's his mother?"

"I don't know," I said.

"Well," Dad said, "I might go and say hello. Coming?"

"I'll wait here."

Dad crossed the road and tapped on the door that had its CLOSED sign showing. I could see Bon's alarmed face, a slice of toast at his mouth. I saw Kelsie wave and grin, open the door, and say hi.

I decided then to follow Dad across the quiet main street, and I stood directly outside the café window.

"Your customer," I heard Dad say. "My nephew. 'Morning, Bon." I saw him ruffle Bon's hair the way he might have done with me, and then have a short conversation I couldn't quite hear. Maybe Bon relaxed a little; he said something to Dad and nodded before taking a long drink from the tall mug that Kelsie had brought to his table. Uncomfortably, he looked at me through the café window.

When Dad returned, he said to me, "*Breakfast.* Kelsie has been giving Bon free breakfasts for a few weeks now. She saw him wandering around early and invited him in. It's a regular thing. Can you believe that? Bon says his mother doesn't have any breakfast to give him; she's asleep when he's ready to go to school." Then Dad asked, "Did you know about this?"

A pause, and then I nodded. "Yes."

"How?"

"I saw him. Other mornings when we were out."

"And you didn't say anything?"

"No," I admitted.

Dad took a deep breath. "Kieran, I think you probably should have. How often have you seen Bon over there?"

"Six, maybe seven times."

Dad exhaled loudly. "Kelsie is not charging him. She's feeding him because she's kind and she cares." He paused. "I thanked her and said she wouldn't have to keep doing it. That Bon and his breakfasts would be looked after from now on."

"Looked after?"

"Renee needs our help," Dad said as he gazed along the length of the main street. "We'll talk about it more at your nan's tonight."

Before I could ask another question, Dad set off jogging. "Come on!" he called.

Somehow I knew I was going to be told something I wasn't going to like, and that it was going to be all about Bon.

He was nowhere to be seen on the playground as the school day dragged on, and I started thinking that maybe Bon and my aunt were gone, had moved away somewhere else.

My aunt's car was not parked outside Nan's house later that day when we arrived. But Bon was curled up on the couch, hypnotized by the television show he was watching. He said hello in a dreamy, absent voice, and I caught sight of his backpack in the spare room, his sneakers and a jacket scattered on the floor. Gina bounced herself down on the couch, alongside Bon.

"Where's Aunt Renee?" I asked, sitting down at the table with Nan and my parents.

"She's already left," Nan said. "She decided to return . . . home."

"Why isn't Bon with her?"

"Because," Nan said, "Bon is staying with me. I had him and Renee here most of the day, which is why he wasn't at school." She paused. "It was good for us three to be together for a while. Kieran, I'm going to be Bon's guardian from now on."

"He's *staying* with you?"

She wants to leave him here with us. Mom had said that the day my aunt had visited, the day Bon had remembered the way to our house. The picture became a little clearer. Bon's mom did not want him, or else could not look after him.

"He's going to stay with you? Why?"

No one answered at first, and the moment of silence quickly became uncomfortable.

"What's the matter with Aunt Renee?" I asked.

"Kieran," Mom began, "Renee is often not an easy person to know or to be with. She doesn't always look after herself, and she never stays in one place very long. She doesn't always make good decisions, and none of that is very good for Bon. Renee knows that, too, and what we've *all* agreed to do is very important. For her, and especially for Bon."

"Kieran," Nan said, "this is not about playing favorites. It's about giving Bon a safe, happy place to be, for as long as he wants. Somewhere to call home."

Home. Reluctantly, I let the word bounce around in my head. "So he's going to live at your house."

"Yes."

"He's going to take over the guest room, so Gina and I can't have sleepovers there anymore."

"You can still have sleepovers." Nan smiled. "Now I have an excuse to clean out the junk room. So there'll be space enough for three grandchildren."

"And," I said, "instead of his mom, it's going to be you looking after him."

"It's what grandparents need to do sometimes, become parents to grandchildren. I know other people my age doing exactly the same."

"You do?" I asked, surprised.

Nan nodded, but I tried to avoid her steady gaze by

focusing on other things—the crimson streaks in her hair, the dangly dragonfly earrings she had chosen to wear that day.

"And it's going to be a team effort," Dad said. "To give your nan a break, we're having Bon stay with us as well. Every second weekend and a couple of weekdays every other week."

It was the last thing I had expected Dad to say, and the surprise must have shown on my face, because Dad added, "We're *all* going to help out. Aren't we, Kieran?"

I couldn't get an answer out. Bon was not only taking over Nan's house, but ours as well. For a moment, I felt like shouting at someone.

Dad thought I was daydreaming. "Kieran?"

"Yeah," I answered doubtfully. "I guess."

Now I'm stuck with him. Now I'm supposed to find a way to like him.

"It's going to be a big change for us all," Mom said, reaching an arm around my shoulders. "Lots of things for us to think about and start getting used to. But it's an even bigger change for Bon."

"We need to tell Gina," Nan said.

"The short, easy version, suitable for six-year-olds," Dad remarked.

Which was how it came out. *Bon is coming to live at Nan's house.*

Bon drifted into the room and was silent. He gazed at the table, the floor, at our night reflections in the kitchen window glass.

"So what are you thinking about all this, Bon?" Mom asked gently.

He was silent a moment longer. "I think it will be good." He used his precise voice, sounding neither happy nor sad. He stood beside where Nan was sitting and leaned against her shoulder.

"What about you, Gina?" Dad asked. "What do you think about Bon living with Nan and staying with us a couple of days each week?"

Gina was happy. When the short, easy version had been told to her, she had jumped up and down a couple of times, exclaiming, "Yay!" She grinned and added, "It's good, because Bon is my favorite cousin."

Bon looked at her. "Thank you," he said, smiling.

Then he looked at me. He held the smile a moment longer before it faded. I could tell he was hoping for me to say something as well, but I couldn't.

It was the longest we had ever faced each other, and the first time I had noticed how long his eyelashes were, and how a little scar above one of his eyes showed as a pale straight line.

I was sitting a long way from everyone, and it was a strange, new experience.

Our SUV had a third, fold-down seat that we only ever used whenever our friends were along for the ride—but now, I had it to myself. My parents were a long way off in the very front, and in the seat behind them were three kids. There was Gina and Emily, because this year it was my sister's turn to choose a friend to come along with us for our one-week vacation at the beach. Last year, I had invited Lucas, only to have Mason find out afterward and say grouchily, "Well, you didn't ask me. That's pretty lame."

"I'll invite you next time," I had reassured him, feeling a bit panicked and awkward. "The year after next."

"What?"

"My sister and I. We take turns; it's like a family rule. Sorry, Mason."

It had been good having Lucas along with us. He behaved differently from the way he did at school — or as I realized, differently from the way he behaved in front of Mason and the other kids. We swam and fished together; he said *thank you* to my parents every time they bought us lunch or dinner, or took us to the movies at the little beachside theater. But with the vacation over and school on again, Lucas went back to his old self.

"Yeah, I had a good time" was all that I heard him say to Mason. Asking him along hadn't turned him into my new best friend. I had started to think hard and worry more about whether even to ask Mason when my turn came around again. Maybe he would be too busy being friends with Lucas — and busy being most popular boy in class — to even remember.

I wriggled down a little farther into my seat and gazed through the window. It was open a bit and the breeze cut sharply across my forehead. I had earphones on and my own music playing. Mom and Dad were talking. I could see Dad relaxed and cheerful, the way he always was at the beginning of a vacation at the beach. On the drive home in a week's time, he would be quieter and maybe even a little disappointed that the trip was over and he would be back working at Rural Engineering soon. But now, I could see a little of his face in the rearview mirror, his eyes hidden behind sunglasses and his teeth occasionally showing, smiling about something Mom was saying. Sometimes his face looked back at mine, or at the loaded trailer we towed behind us.

In a long meandering line, the back road across to the ocean passed dry yellow fields and slopes, deserted farmhouses, and grazing sheep. Gradually, the hills bunched up and became greener, and the open country became shaded with trees and bushes. There was a place where we would reach the top of the mountain range and begin the steep downhill run, where the coast would start to appear in promising glimpses and the air would start to smell a little of salt water.

In the row in front of me, Gina's and Emily's heads were tilted at the same angle. They had talked and giggled nonstop for the first hour of the journey, and then fallen soundly asleep. The third kid in the middle row was still awake.

It was Bon, and I had done my best to pretend he wasn't there at all, or at least to ignore him. From the angle of his head, I could tell he was reading, or maybe drawing his stupid pictures or maps. He wore a set of earphones, bought by Nan, and was listening to music he had downloaded from her computer.

"I should have rented a bus," Dad had remarked back at home.

"We couldn't just leave him," Mom had said. "The choice was with us, or have him be the only boy in a busload of grandmas and aunties. What eleven-year-old boy would find *that* fun?"

Bon, probably, I thought bitterly, wishing that Nan's trip to the city with her golfing friends wasn't happening at the same time as our only vacation away for the year. I would have loved the thought of Bon being dragged along on shopping trips, river cruises, or horse-racing days with Nan. There could have been no better revenge.

"He's probably never seen the beach," Dad had replied.

"He's probably never been away on a vacation," Mom had pointed out gently.

I didn't feel sorry for Bon. In the car now, I glared at the back of his head, at his braid pulled sideways and spilling down against his own window. I knew I didn't want to be seen anywhere at the beach alongside him, that there would be plenty of other kids at the motel to make friends and hang out with. I squirmed at the thought of Bon with his stupid braid, with the babyish wool hat I'd seen packed in his overnight bag, along with the new clothes that Mom and Nan had been buying him. Instead of having my own room at the motel, I'd be sharing with the last person I would have chosen to invite.

When we arrived, there were no other kids my age at the motel. It seemed to be nothing but little girls the same age as Gina and Emily, or else teenagers with sunglasses and loud voices. I sat miserably through an hour of boring afternoon television while Bon and the girls swam in the motel pool with Mom. I would have scowled my way through our first night there and through dinner at the local restaurant, except for one thing the waitress said. She was about to take our meal orders and looked first at the side of the table where Gina, Emily, and Bon all sat beside one another. "Are you three girls ready to order?" she asked.

I laughed out loud. Mom nudged me with her elbow and whispered my name in an annoyed voice. Out of the corner of one eye, I could see Dad looking down at the table and grinning to himself.

"*Two* girls," Gina explained to the waitress. "Me and my friend Emily are girls. And this is Bon. He's a boy and he's my cousin. He's been growing his hair for *four* years!"

"My mistake. I'm so sorry," the waitress said to Bon, and I could tell she was really embarrassed.

Bon simply shrugged his shoulders and replied, "I'd like salt-and-pepper squid, please. With fries and salad."

Afterward, with our food in front of us, I asked, "Hey, are you three girls enjoying your meals?" Mom elbowed me again, frowning and shaking her head.

But Bon was going to give me at least one other thing to laugh about.

Dad and I liked to go fishing along the deepwater jetty at the end of the bay. It was one of the places we visited each year we came to the coast. Mom wasn't the fishing type. "It's like watching paint dry," she remarked, although she was happy to barbecue and eat whatever we caught when we had evening picnics at the beachside park, along with other vacationing families. So Dad and I took our rods, bucket, and gear to the jetty while Mom took the girls to the beach and the rock pools at the opposite end of the bay. Except this time, it wasn't just Dad and me—Bon came along, too. I didn't know why, because everything about fishing seemed to worry or scare him.

"Doesn't it hurt the fish?" he asked.

"A little, I guess," Dad replied as he and I baited up our hooks and checked our rods.

"But when you catch a fish, what happens then?" Bon asked.

"If it's too small, or it's a protected species, we let it go," Dad told him. "If it's big enough, and it's what we're after, it goes into the catch bucket."

"Do you *eat* it?"

"Sure do," Dad told him.

"But there's . . . cutting up," Bon said, and he sounded really worried. "Who does that?"

"I do," Dad said. "I can show you how if you—"

"No!" Bon almost shouted, and moved a little away from us. He watched in silence as we sent our lines swishing into the water below the jetty, and then he sat down, pulling his cloth cap over his face so that I couldn't quite see his eyes.

"Scaredy-cat," I mumbled, hoping Dad might agree.

"He's OK," Dad said. "This is all kind of new to him."

After a while, Bon hovered closer and Dad offered him a turn fishing with his rod. "But you hold it good and tight," Dad said firmly, though he smiled as well. "Because if you drop my rod, you're going in after it. I assume you know how to swim, Bon."

"I'm a good swimmer," Bon replied. I wondered how much of a fib he was telling. "And if I catch anything, I'm throwing it back. I don't want my fish killed."

Dad and I laughed. "It'll be your fish and your decision," Dad told him.

In the end, Bon didn't catch anything, but he sat for quite a long time with Dad's rod, gazing out at the water and humming to himself. I thought I saw the rod twitch one time, but Bon didn't flick the rod back or wind the line in. Eventually, he decided he'd had enough of a turn. The bait was well and truly gone when the hook came spinning shinily from the deep water below.

Between us, Dad and I caught five fish. Bon turned away each time we caught something, and he refused to look into the catch bucket, or go anywhere near us as Dad and I scaled and filleted our catch at the preparation benches near the jetty bait shop. And when we had dinner at the beachside barbecue area, I saw Bon avoiding the fish and eating only the salads Mom had prepared.

It had been a good second day, and when we returned to the motel, we all went for a sunset swim in the heated pool. Except for Bon, who shook his head and went back to our room.

"He's fine," Mom said to no one in particular. "I imagine he wants to watch television or draw in his book."

His stupid book of maps and inventions, I thought. *Waste of paper.*

But I knew Bon was trying to hide something the moment I walked back into our room. He hunched over his bedspread, scrunching the covers into an awkward handful.

"What are you doing?" I demanded. "What have you got?"

"Nothing."

"Liar," I replied, and pulled the bedspread from his grasp. I was stronger than he was, and the covers came half off the bed, spilling the hidden contents onto the floor. Just as before, they were figures from my medieval castle. "You thief!" I shouted.

Mom was in the doorway. "What's going on?" she asked.

"Him," I said, scowling at Bon. "He's been sneaking around my room at home again. He's taken things without asking."

"Those?" Mom asked, pointing at the figures—the same white horse and the same knight with the blue crested flag that Bon had taken two years ago. There was another knight as well this time—and the princess with her conical hat and long red gown. "Did you take those without asking, Bon?"

"Yes," I answered, because Bon, looking guiltily at Mom, said nothing.

Mom glared at me a moment and then looked back at Bon. "I'm asking you a question, Bon. What's the answer?"

"If I'd asked," Bon replied, "Kieran would have said no."

Mom sighed, and then lectured Bon about not helping himself to things that weren't his. "And now that you've got them, I'd like you to say something to Kieran."

Bon looked up quickly. "I'm sorry," he said to me.

I scowled back at him.

After a pause, he asked, "But can I borrow them? Just till we go home?"

In the dark after bedtime, I hissed, "You take my things without asking, and you barge in on our family vacation. I wish you weren't my cousin and I wish I didn't know you." I heaved a long, angry breath, and then waited in silence, wondering if Bon would reply or not. Keeping still, I realized I could hear him whispering to himself, the way I'd heard him do at home. It went on for a long time, until I interrupted. "Say it out loud to me. I dare you."

The whispering stopped, and for a moment there was silence.

Then Bon said in a quiet voice, "I'm sorry about being here. But my mom can't look after me. It's too hard for her."

I wasn't sure how to reply to that. His answer unsettled me in a way I couldn't quite explain, so instead I listened as his breathing slowed into the steady softness that told me he was sleeping.

For the rest of that week, I did my best to avoid wherever Bon would be, which was easy at least some of the time. He didn't come fishing with me and Dad anymore, preferring to stay with Mom and the girls, exploring the rock pools or walking around the beach-side shops. Once or twice, I walked into our bedroom to find Bon kneeling with his drawing book at the foot of his bed. He had the bedspread bunched up and my medieval figures arranged across the folds. I pretended not to be interested, but I realized what he was seeing and drawing when I stopped in the door-way to look more carefully. The folds of the bedspread were a landscape of hills and valleys that the knights on horseback were traveling across. On a distant hill-top, the princess in her gown and cape waited and watched.

I waited until Bon was outside in the motel swim-ming pool before quickly searching his overnight bag and pulling out his maps and inventions book. Soon enough, I found the page he'd been working on, and there was the bedspread landscape as a story picture, together with a paragraph scrawled underneath in Bon's messy handwriting.

Bon the Crusader and Kieran the Brave have journeyed

to the ocean's edge. Back at the village, Julia the Fair is preparing for her own journey.

I read it twice, annoyed and embarassed to see my own name mentioned. For a moment, I toyed with the idea of tearing the page out, but instead closed the book and shoved it back into his bag before deciding to go for a swim as well.

The pool was fairly crowded with other people staying at the motel. Gina and Emily were playing some kind of chasing game at the shallow end with a bunch of other little girls. Mom was in the middle of the pool, trying to keep away from all the splashing at the shallow end, and was talking with another parent. Bon was up near where the kids were playing and whooping. He wasn't part of any game or group, and he wasn't doing much of anything. I'd heard Mom tell Dad the day before, "Bon's actually a really good swimmer. I'm surprised. Where would he have learned?"

Because I'd been doing my best to stay away from him, I hadn't seen any evidence of this fantastic talent. Maybe Mom was trying to find nice things about Bon, and a bit of leg kicking and dog-paddling passed for good swimming.

I found an empty patch of pool, dived in, and swam to one end, thinking it might be possible to do some laps without bumping into annoying little kids or, worst of all, Bon. I knew I could show him a thing or two about swimming because, like Gina, I had learned before even starting school.

"Ten laps," I murmured, wiping the comfortably warm water from my face. "Too easy." The pool was short, and ten times would be, I guessed, about two hundred yards. I launched myself away.

And it *was* easy. I managed one, two, three laps without a pause and without anyone else getting in the way. At the third turnaround I glanced sideways and found that Bon had moved across to my part of the pool.

"Keep out of the way," I muttered quickly at him, before setting off for lap number four. But when I returned next and set off on lap number six, Bon launched himself off beside me. Trying to ignore him, I focused on my stroke and speed, but knew by quick glimpses and the close sound of his own hands and feet splashing in the water that he was keeping up with me. Bon *could* swim.

"Stop following me," I told him, feeling both surprised and annoyed.

"I'm not following you," he replied. "I'm just swimming."

Without saying any more, I launched myself into lap number seven. And so did Bon, who kept up with me again, all the way to the other end of the pool.

We stopped next to the tiled edge and looked at each other. Bon wiped water from his face. His braid half floated in the water behind him and his mouth was open a little, as though he were at a loss for something to say.

I wasn't. Against the noise of little girls shrieking and splashing, I asked, "Who taught *you* to swim?"

Bon hesitated. "Sam," he answered at last.

I remembered Bon at Dad's soccer practice. *Which one is Sam?* "Who are you talking about?" I demanded.

"Someone my mom used to know. When I was little."

"You mean a boyfriend — that guy with the black pickup."

"No," Bon answered abruptly. "That was *Brian*." He said the name as though spitting it out. "Sam taught me how to swim. He was nice, but Mom . . ." He looked away from me, as though distracted.

"Yeah — what?"

"Nothing."

I wanted to finish my laps, but had something else to say, something else to make him feel awkward. "Where is Julia the Fair going?" I asked.

Bon blinked in surprise. "Why did you look in my book?"

"Because I wanted to see what you were writing and

drawing. And anyway, I've looked at it before—Bon the Crusader."

He paused. "It's just a story I'm writing and drawing. It's imaginary."

"But parts of it are real—the names. And I'm in the story, too. How come I'm Kieran the Brave?"

"Because," Bon answered, sounding embarrassed, "I think you are. And it suits the story character. That's all."

"That's stupid," I sneered. "I don't want to be Kieran the anything. That's so lame. Anyway, are you going to keep writing and drawing it, now that I've seen it?"

Bon looked steadily at me. Dribbles of pool water were still running down his face, and he wiped them away with one hand. "Yes," he answered. "It's not a story unless it's finished and the adventure has a proper ending."

"How's the story going to end?" I put on a squeaky voice to add, *"They all lived happily ever after."*

"It might be like that. I don't know yet."

"So," I said, "you don't know where Julia is going yet? In the story?"

"No. Not yet. I have to wait and see."

"I bet you miss your girlfriend," I said sarcastically, "being this far away on your free vacation."

After a pause, he answered. "Yes." Then he said, "Are you missing her, too?"

Before I could think of something to say, he dropped down beneath the water and I saw him move swiftly across the bottom of the pool toward the steps. He knew I wouldn't want him to hear my answer. And he knew the answer would be, *Yes, I miss her.*

Bon had set off for school with us that morning looking clean and tidy. He came home looking exactly the opposite, his hair half undone and his clothes looking grimy.

"What happened?" Mom asked as soon as she saw him. "It looks like you've been caught in a hurricane!"

Bon shrugged and didn't say anything about how, on the playground, Mason had yanked on his braid so hard that Bon's hair elastic had sprung loose. His braid had unraveled and he hadn't been able to get it quite right again afterward. Bon also didn't say anything about how his new school shirt had lost two buttons. That had been Lucas heaving Bon out of his place in the lunch line.

"Some boys in Kieran's class were annoying Bon," Gina reported. "I saw them and told the teacher."

"Is that so?" Mom asked Bon. She looked at me. "Did you see any of this, Kieran?"

"I thought they were playing a game," I said, hoping it sounded like an innocent reply.

I could tell from her expression that Mom guessed there might be more to the story. She pointed to the kitchen stool. "Come and sit down," she told Bon.

The ritual of Bon and his hair usually took place each school morning that he was with us. It would always be Gina first, with her request for ponytails, braids, or something more complicated, and then Bon. Mom usually had his braid done quickly, but this afternoon she worked more slowly. She pulled his hair loose and took some time brushing it out. She stopped and stood back for a moment, telling him, "You look like you've stepped out of a medieval castle."

Bon looked pleased about that. "Do I?" He looked straight at her and smiled a little.

I rolled my eyes and shook my head before raiding the fruit bowl on the kitchen island. Noisily, I crunched an apple and silently watched all the attention Mom was giving Bon. The braid had curled his hair, and it dropped in curtains past his shoulders. His face seemed smaller and younger with his hair down.

"But your ends are all split," Mom told him. She picked up strands of hair and looked at them closely. "Will you let me give you a trim?"

Bon looked doubtful. "What do you mean?" he asked cautiously.

"Just the ends," Mom explained. "No more than an inch off."

Bon frowned.

Mom laughed. "I promise! Trust me, Bon. Didn't your mom ever get someone to cut them?"

"No," Bon answered in a flat voice. "But she taught me how to braid."

Mom turned to me. "Kieran, make yourself useful. Go and get me the hairdressing scissors from the bathroom. You know where they're kept."

Of course I knew where they were kept. And knowing how to keep Bon feeling nervous, I came back with the blades loudly clicking open and shut in the air above my head. "Let *me* help!" I offered, using my best Crazy Guy voice. "*I'll* cut Bon's hair! I'm *good* at cutting hair!" And I clacked the scissor blades loudly again for extra effect.

Bon jumped off the stool and looked ready to run out the back door.

"Kieran," Mom scolded. "Give me the scissors and then go and do something else. Like homework, which I know you've got in your bag."

"Bon's got homework as well."

"And he'll be doing his shortly. Go away and stop

causing trouble. Bon, come sit down again. I'm the only hairdresser in this household, so you can ignore your cousin, who's just going off to do his homework. *Now.*"

Bon stared at me for a moment more, as though I had another pair of scissors hidden in my hand and was ready to give him a buzz cut. Then he edged back to the stool and sat down again.

"Homework, Kieran," Mom said.

"Yeah, yeah, I'm going," I answered wearily. As I walked away, I heard her say to Bon, "Do you want to tell me what really happened at school today?"

I was grateful for the peace and quiet of my room, to know that I had it to myself for at least a little while, without Bon fidgeting in the background. Even if he had left his clothes and, worst of all, yesterday's underwear, lying all over the carpet. When I thought I'd spent enough time on the math and language assignments Mr. Garcia had given us, I walked back up the hallway.

I could hear Bon's voice. His own homework was spread across the kitchen table, but he was standing over at the kitchen island, next to Mom. Or rather, he was leaning—not against the island, but against Mom, as though expecting a hug. And he was reading from one of her cookbooks.

His voice sounded different as he did this—confident, I realized, which surprised me.

It had the same effect on Mom, because she suddenly told him, "Bon, you're a good reader. Really good."

"It's because I practice," he told her, as though stating an obvious fact.

"I mean it," she answered. "I thought it'd be something you'd have trouble with. Going to so many different schools can affect the way kids learn sometimes. How many schools have you been to?"

He shrugged. "I don't know. A few."

Mom paused and looked at Bon for what seemed like a very long time. "Well," she said at last, "you can read to me anytime you like. OK?" And she let the arm Bon was nestling under wrap around his shoulder in the hug I guessed he'd been hoping for.

"OK," he answered. His hair was brushed and neatly braided, and he would have looked pleased if he hadn't seen me back in the kitchen again. I looked at his homework and made a face. He really did have the messiest writing I'd ever seen. It was scrawled over the lines and answer spaces in a way that I could barely read.

"That looks really gross," I remarked. "It's like a two-year-old snuck in and scribbled all over the page."

"Bon's finished his homework for Miss McLennan. How's your homework, Kieran?"

"All done," I answered. "And it's *really* neat. As usual."

Mom smiled at Bon. "Put your things away, and

then it's your choice for half an hour before dinner—computer or television." As he slipped away, Mom turned to me. "You and I need to go outside for a little while. We need to talk."

As soon as we were on the back deck, Mom sat down on a bench and had me sit beside her. "Kieran," she said, "you're not being very nice to Bon."

I was expecting a scolding, not this quiet voice.

"No," I admitted.

"Like we said, this is a big change—for all of us. And I can tell you're not finding it so easy." Mom waited for me to say something, but when I didn't, she continued. "As your nan put it, this is not about playing favorites. It's about giving Bon somewhere he feels safe and somewhere he can be happy. Everybody deserves that, and it's something Bon needs very much."

"Why does he have to sleep in my room?"

"We've been through this before. He's your cousin. And now he's very much a part of our lives. You need to share and give a little, Kieran."

"Why can't Gina and I take turns, then? Or he can go sleep in the shed; Dad's got a couch there."

"With the lawn mower, the tools, and the beer fridge?" She almost laughed at that. "Kieran, our house is just not big enough for him to be anywhere else. Gina's room is smaller than yours. Bon would have trouble finding space on the floor among all the dolls and toy ponies. Would *you* like to sleep in there?"

"No," I snorted.

"It's going to be a special thing for Bon to get to know us properly. There's probably a great deal he hasn't had in his life. He and you are the same age, and I think there's nothing he'd like more than for you to be more than a cousin to him."

"What do you mean?" I asked, looking down at the deck.

"Be a friend, Kieran."

The silence that followed seemed to last for minutes. I could have stood up and stomped inside, making sure to slam the screen door as I went. But Mom rested one hand lightly on my shoulder, as though anchoring me for something more.

"It's been quite a while since you've had a friend over to visit or spend the night. Like Mason or Lucas, for instance. Is there a reason for that?"

I shrugged and said nothing.

"Is the reason anything to do with Connor?"

I sighed. "Please, Mom—"

"I know you miss him."

Now I wanted to escape this conversation. "Is that all you needed to say to me?"

Mom squeezed my shoulder; it made me turn and

face her. "You've always been kind and considerate," she said. "I don't want that to change. Please be patient and show Bon a little more understanding. OK?"

I nodded. "Yeah," I mumbled, knowing the sound of my voice would be telling Mom I hadn't really changed my mind at all.

I ignored Bon and ate in silence throughout dinner. Afterward, I sat as far away from him as I could to watch television.

My bedroom faced toward the sunset, but the sky had darkened early with gray clouds and it had begun to rain. I lay very still in bed, enjoying the rattle of rain on the roof. Imagining that Bon was not here in my room, I willed myself to fall asleep.

Bon tossed and turned. His sheets rustled; his feet stretched and kicked so that the trundle bed creaked and moved.

"The rain on the roof," he said at last. "It sounds like voices."

"*What?*" I grumbled.

"Voices," Bon repeated. "Men's voices, like there's a bunch of them talking. Listen."

It was a trick, that soft noise of water falling onto tin. And the darkness was a trick as well, the way it made the shape and feel of things change. So although

I wanted to pretend to be scornful of anything that Bon said, I listened carefully. I wanted to be able to tell him, *Nonsense,* because what he was hearing was really the sound of the television in the living room, or maybe some of the neighbors out on their back porch having a conversation. It was neither. There *was* the sound of voices in the raindrops hitting the roof. I remembered thinking of it like that long ago, when I was younger. But I wouldn't tell that to Bon.

"I can't hear anything but rain," I said. "You're being weird."

In the darkness came a sigh. "There is, you know. You just have to listen."

"Shut up. Go to sleep."

But he didn't, and so neither did I. He rustled and moved, he rolled over onto his stomach, then onto his back. Whenever I thought I felt my mind and body slowing and my eyes closing, I could hear that Bon was still awake. Beyond my room, Mom and Dad switched off the television and the lights, ran a tap and brushed teeth, and murmured their voices along the hallway and behind the closed door of their bedroom. Everything in the house became still. Except for Bon.

Finally, I became too fed up. I desperately wanted to sleep, so, picking up my pillow and blanket, I left Bon to his tossing and turning.

"Where are you going?" I heard him ask behind me, but I ignored him and walked in bare feet to the living room, hoping he wouldn't follow and that my parents wouldn't hear me and make a fuss. I sank into the sofa cushions, pulled the blanket over my head, and fell asleep very quickly.

I woke again to the same stillness and darkness. I spent a while thinking and hoping that Bon would finally be asleep, before padding back to my room and finding the outline of my bed.

I was wrong. As I settled down under my own blankets again, I could see him. He was kneeling up on the trundle bed now, perfectly still and quiet. From the moonlight that shone through the window, I could see his hair a little frizzed and messed up. He was gazing out the window, and from behind, it was hard to know exactly what he was looking at: Our backyard? The neighbors' houses? The town? The moonlight showing through the last of the rain clouds? I wondered for a moment if he was even fully awake.

"Go to sleep," I grumbled, but it was as though Bon didn't hear.

In the morning, he was awake before me, sitting on his bed and still looking outside. I couldn't tell if he'd slept at all.

* * *

Usually, I slept soundly.

"Thunderstorms, explosions, rock concerts," Dad had told Ant and Split Pin one afternoon down at the Guys' Room, "Kieran could sleep right through it all without batting an eyelid."

But I wasn't sleeping like that whenever Bon came to stay. Having him share my room changed everything.

After lights-out, he would fidget and be restless; he seemed to stay awake a long time. I began to sense that he was not only awake, but out of bed during the night—and not just for a walk down the hallway for a pee, either. Once I woke to see Mom guiding Bon back into my bedroom. He shuffled like a sleepwalker, and Mom sat down on the mattress beside him for a while, stroking his forehead and resting a hand on his shoulder as he lay back under the blankets.

Another time, I woke to see his shadowed shape standing at the window, and I was sure that he was wearing sneakers and outdoor clothes. When I heard his fingers picking at the window latch, I woke enough to whisper, "What are you doing?"

He jumped and I heard his breath catch.

"What are you doing?" I hissed. "Go back to bed. And don't touch any of my things, either."

I had surprised Bon enough to make him not say a word in reply. In the moments that followed, I heard him get quickly back into his bed, with more rustling and fussing than usual.

"Stop making so much noise," I hissed again, sure that he was wriggling out of shoes and clothing under the covers. Where had he been about to go? "I'm telling Mom on you," I added. "I'm sick of you and your noise."

"It's not fair," I told her the next day. "He keeps me awake."

Mom was busy with Gina and Bon, attending to braids and ponytails. Our three lunch boxes were lined up on the kitchen island, ready for school.

"I don't keep you awake," said Bon in a flat voice. He avoided looking at me.

"You do. He does, Mom." I wondered whether to mention being certain that Bon had not only been awake this time, but dressed in more than pajamas.

"Are you still having trouble sleeping?" Mom asked Bon.

"He's *never* still," I continued. "I can hear him. It's like he does it on purpose."

Mom glared at me. I glared at Bon, and this time he looked at me, guilty and uncomfortable.

"I don't," he protested again. "Usually, I don't go to bed so early," he added, and then corrected himself. "I *used* to not go to bed so early."

"How late was your bedtime?" Mom asked.

"Midnight. And sometimes I stayed up nearly all night if there was good stuff on television."

"Sure," I said, disbelieving.

"It's true," he answered, and I could hear that he wasn't boasting. I knew it probably was a truth that belonged to whatever life Bon had led before he'd come to live at Nan's house and started the regular sleepovers with us.

All the things I'd heard about my aunt and Bon were beginning to piece themselves together into a jigsaw puzzle, and now there were more pieces that fit— the faded clothing Bon had first arrived in; Kelsie Graney giving him free café breakfasts; a camper at the trailer park to call home, and then a room at the Imperial Hotel.

"Sometimes," Bon added, "my mom wouldn't sleep. I had to stay awake to make sure that she was OK."

There was another puzzle piece: the sight of my aunt's hand clenching Bon's face tightly as he looked away, pretending that nothing was wrong. I flinched as though the pain had found my own face. In that moment, I felt a cloud of anger drift away, and knew something I wasn't ready to admit out loud.

I felt sorry for my cousin.

The skirt was Mason's idea, but as soon as I laughed, it felt as though it had almost become my idea as well. I felt guilty and reluctant, but for Mason, the tripping, hair pulling, and name-calling was getting boring. And one day at the lost and found near the school office, when Mason retrieved the jacket he'd left on the playground the previous day, he found one of the girls' sports skirts as well. It had AMBER HODGES printed clearly on the inside name tag, but Mason wasn't about to let Amber know right away that he had it.

"Wait till he's over near the bathroom," Mason said to us during the first half of lunch. We had our sandwiches and drinks balanced in our laps, and Mason had the sports skirt neatly folded and hidden. "He'll have to go sooner or later. Then surround him and kind of walk him inside so that the teacher on playground duty doesn't notice."

Lucas interrupted. "It's Miss Perez today. She's always got tons of little kids following her around. She won't notice right away."

"If a couple of us grab him," Mason continued, "and hold him still where the sinks are, we can get the skirt on him. Then walk him back out to the playground—and run. Leave him where everyone can see. It'll be hilarious."

"Have you got your phone in your bag?" Brendan Ashcroft asked. "You could take photos as well."

I listened, feeling more and more uneasy.

"What if he tells on us?" Ethan Coulter said.

"He won't tell; he never does. He's a weakling."

"What if he kicks and shouts and stuff, when you're trying to get the skirt on him?"

"So it'll take three of you to hold him and keep him quiet. Put your hand over his mouth," said Mason.

"He might bite."

"He won't. Probably wet his pants, like a baby. Someone needs to guard the doorway, keep little kids out and be a lookout in case the teacher gets close." Mason turned to me. "How come you're not saying anything? *You* have to be part of it, Kieran. You can be on lookout duty."

"We shouldn't do it," I said. "We'll get caught. Tons of kids will see what's happening and tell the teachers."

"Are you protecting him because he's your cousin?" Mason sneered.

"You're going to get caught," I repeated. "It's not worth it."

"You're being gutless," Lucas said. "Your cousin's a freak, and you don't want to be part of a prank."

"Taking photos with your phone is a really bad idea," I added, a little desperately. Now, as I pictured the whole thing in my head — almost imagining myself as Bon being treated in this way — a thread of determination crept into my voice. "A whole bunch of kids against one isn't fair. Don't do it."

"You thought it was a funny idea five minutes ago," Brendan said. "Now you're trying to wriggle out of it."

"You're lookout," Mason reminded me.

Unhappily, I looked around the group. Mason, Lucas, and Brendan were exchanging knowing smiles. Ethan and Liam didn't seem quite as sure, but I sensed they'd simply follow whatever the other three said and did.

"I don't want to be lookout. I don't think you should do any of this," I said, but no one seemed to be listening.

The bell for recess rang, and kids everywhere stood up, took lunch trash to the bins, and ran off to play. Other boys had overheard by now, and they followed Mason and Lucas across the playground.

"Don't try to get out of it," Mason warned me. "You've told us before how you don't like him. Here's a chance to let him know how no one here likes him."

"This isn't fair," I said, my voice raised. "Eight kids against just one."

Mason paused and looked me up and down. His face read *coward*. He turned and walked away with the others. I could see Bon walking toward the basketball hoops with Julia and the girls. They passed quite close to where I was still standing, and I tried to catch Bon's eye, shaking my head slightly and mouthing a warning. But he wasn't paying attention. Mason, Lucas, and the other boys took up a position near—but not too close to—the bathroom, and they put on a show of small talk, all the while glancing over to where Bon and the girls were playing, as well as keeping an eye on the playground-duty teacher. Uncomfortably, I stood at the edge of my group, not really taking any notice of the silly stuff being said.

"Don't forget, you're lookout," Mason said once more, and I tried to ignore that, too, hoping that Miss Perez would happen to walk over and make us all go away somewhere else. But it was no use. Time dragged on until finally I knew that lunchtime play was going to end soon. And just as I was afraid he would, Bon had left the girls and was walking toward us. *Stay away. Wait till the bell rings.* But he walked on, closer and closer, until he came to where the group stood. It all happened quickly, and just as Mason and Lucas had planned it. Bon was grabbed by the arms and led into where the sinks were.

I was *not* going to be the lookout.

Too late, I turned and ran, hoping to reach the spot on the playground where Miss Perez and her usual group of little followers were. But Julia and her friends were closer.

"It's Bon," I said to her, pointing behind me. "Mason, Lucas, the other boys—" I couldn't get an explanation out quickly enough.

Julia knew immediately that something bad was happening. Without saying a word, she sprinted across the playground at the very moment that Bon was pushed out.

The boys had put Amber Hodges's sports skirt over the top of the track pants that Bon had worn to school, and now he was frantically picking at the zipper to get rid of it. Someone had pulled his hair undone so that it spilled over his shoulders in a tangle. He kicked the skirt off and stared at the ground. I found it hard to look at him.

"Leave him alone!" Julia shouted, pushing through

the group of kids that had gathered around to join in the shouting and cheering. "You boys are being really mean!"

Mason put on a silly voice. "Ooh, sorry, Mommy."

"You're a freak," Brendan told Bon as kids kept laughing and pointing.

"Yeah," Mason repeated, "a freak. Go and find some other freaks to be your friend. Like Julia the freak." He looked at me. "Or Kieran the coward."

Bon stared wordlessly at everybody, the sports skirt crumpled at his feet.

"You're the cowards," Julia said, and something in her voice made the shouting and noise fade.

"Loser," Ethan said, filling the sudden quiet.

The word hung heavily in the air between us for a moment, before Mason said, "C'mon, everyone. Let's go join the normal kids."

At that moment came Miss Perez's loud, sharp voice. "All of you boys stay right where you are. All of you!"

We were all sent to sit against the library wall at the edge of the playground, and at lining-up time, Miss Perez stood at the front of all the kids in their class groups and said, in the unfriendliest voice I'd ever heard her use, "Both fifth-grade classes are to remain seated and wait behind. Mrs. Gallagher is coming out to speak with you."

"Oh, *great*," I heard Brendan say as the other classes turned to stare at us. They were standing up and beginning to follow their teachers away toward the classrooms. "Busted, big-time."

"Thanks a lot, boys," said Lucy McDonald, and a chorus of girls joined in, annoyed that everyone seemed to be in trouble. Our teachers glared at us and told us to keep the noise down, but the angry comments and whispers continued.

I had sat myself away from Mason and Lucas, so that Bon and Julia were sitting in front of me, uncomfortably close. Bon sat perfectly still, his head lowered and his hand moving slightly as he scratched a small stick into a gap in the playground concrete. Julia sat facing me.

"Did you say *anything* to those boys to make them stop?" she asked, her voice both soft and fierce.

"I tried to," I whispered back. "I really tried. But they wouldn't listen."

"You have to do more than try," she replied quietly. "You have show them you're on Bon's side. What if I'm not always here? Who's going to stand up for him then?"

If I'm not always here? I looked at her closely. "What do you mean?" I asked, but Julia did not reply. "I knew it wasn't fair," I mumbled, looking down, wondering if

Bon was overhearing any of this. He was still scratching the ground with his stick.

"Sure," Julia said, "but next time you have to do more. And it has to be for always." She paused. "Kieran? Promise."

I sensed that this was my last chance to let her know that I was someone to trust and like. I nodded, a mixture of *yes* and *promise*. Anything I might have said out loud was interrupted by the arrival of Mrs. Gallagher.

Our principal was furious. "I will not have this sort of bullying in our school," she thundered. "It's a disgraceful way to treat a fellow pupil." The beads on her bracelet rattled as she moved a hand in time to each word.

Everyone was very still and silent. We were the oldest pupils in the school, Mrs. Gallagher told us. We had a responsibility to set a good example to the younger children. It was expected of us, she said, that we respect every member of the school and one another's differences and individuality. The playground, Mrs. Gallagher reminded us, was a place where everyone had a right to feel safe and happy. And then came the part I expected. "Those boys responsible for today's incident on the playground are now going to take responsibility for their actions. Stand up if you were involved."

For a moment, nothing happened. Kids exchanged

glances, and the girls turned and frowned at the boys, mostly at Mason and Lucas. Mrs. Gallagher glared at everybody in our two classes and waited.

Slowly, I stood up. A puzzled look seemed to cross Mrs. Gallagher's face for a moment, but she quickly resumed her cranky glare. After what felt like a long wait, Mason, Lucas, Brendan, Ethan, and Liam stood up, followed by a few other boys who'd joined in.

Somehow, Mrs. Gallagher seemed to know that there was no one else. She stepped close to where Bon and Julia sat. "Bon," she said quietly. "Would you like to come over and talk to me about what happened?"

Bon, still looking down, shook his head.

"When you feel ready, I'd really like to hear your point of view. And it would be good for these boys to hear from you, as well," said Mrs. Gallagher.

I looked at Bon, and then at Julia. I saw that she was smiling, and that Bon had dropped the stick. His arms were folded close to his chest.

It was a long afternoon. Because I had been first to stand up, and probably because I was related to Bon, Mrs. Gallagher spoke to me in her office first.

"How do you feel about what happened to your cousin, Kieran?" she asked.

"Not very good," I admitted.

"Was there anything you could have done to keep it from happening?"

"Probably." I sighed. "I should have told a teacher right away what the boys were planning."

"Yes," she agreed firmly. "And does Bon deserve an apology, do you think?"

I nodded.

"I'd like you to write that down," Mrs. Gallagher said. "Think about how all of this has happened, and write that down as well. And about how to make sure that it doesn't happen again. OK?"

Mason, Lucas, and the other kids were all lined up in the hallway as I left the principal's office. I avoided looking at them as I walked to the empty office next door. There were a couple of pens and a notepad, which I stared at for quite some time, unable to think of what to write. From next door, I heard the sounds of Mrs. Gallagher's voice, mumbles from Mason, Lucas, and some of the other boys. I heard them being told to go back to class and write out what had happened as well. Then I could hear Mrs. Gallagher phoning parents. "Mrs. Cutler," I heard her begin. She made other phone calls as well, and I figured she would call my house, that I was facing trouble when I arrived home from school. Afterward, there was a stretch of silence beyond the room where I sat, except for the nearby hum and click of the office photocopier.

Then I heard Julia's voice.

"Mrs. Gallagher, you know it wasn't just today that those boys have picked on Bon."

"Julia," came the reassuring reply, "I know, and it's being dealt with. Why are you out of class?"

"Because Bon is my friend."

I stared at the blank notepad page a bit more, and I began to write. *Because Bon was a new kid,* I wrote, *and because he looked unusual is why a lot of the boys started picking on him.* I thought a moment, and added, *Even me.*

The hum of voices from the principal's office echoed softly between the open doorways. Then came something I heard more clearly.

"Julia, the school your mother wrote down as being your last school — on the enrollment forms —"

"It was out of state, ma'am."

"I know that. I contacted them and they had no record of you being there. Can you tell me the school you last attended, Julia?"

Julia's reply was a place I had never heard of.

I heard Mrs. Gallagher's voice. "It's just that I feel I need to rely on you for answers, rather than your mother. Something here is not quite right." There was a long moment of silence before she spoke again. "Julia, do you and your mother move around a lot?"

"Yes," Julia replied after a pause.

"Is there a reason for that?"

"My mom doesn't want my dad to find me."

I could hear the sigh in Mrs. Gallagher's voice. "Julia, you understand that I have to take a step away from this. It needs to be put into someone else's hands. You might need help that I'm not in a position to give."

"But I'm OK for now," Julia said. "I'm totally fine. It's Bon that you need to help. Not me."

Mrs. Gallagher's voice dropped to a confidential murmur.

Julia murmured a reply, then said, "Thank you, ma'am," in a louder voice I thought sounded pleased. And suddenly, she was in the doorway of the room where I sat. "Hi," she whispered.

"Hi," I whispered back, surprised.

"What are you writing?"

"About what happened at lunchtime. And the times before."

"You stood up first. I liked how you did that."

It sounded like a compliment. A little relieved, I shrugged.

"Those boys will leave Bon alone now," Julia said.

We looked at each other for an awkward moment,

and I could almost sense she knew I had been listening to her conversation with Mrs. Gallagher. "I heard what you said," I told her with an effort. "About your mom. And your dad."

Julia nodded slowly.

"I won't tell anyone else," I said.

"I know you won't," Julia whispered. She was silent for a moment. "See you after school," she said at last.

"See you," I replied, and heard her footsteps sounding away along the corridor.

I haven't had a school photo for two years. Julia had said that to her mom that afternoon at the supermarket.

My mom doesn't want my dad to find me. I had just heard her say that to our school principal. I stared at my writing, my head full all over again with the mystery of Julia and her life, about how she had arrived in town at the same time as Bon.

I managed to finish writing. *I am sorry about Bon being treated badly and will help it never to happen again.*

I showed Mrs. Gallagher my page and wondered why she'd kept me here when the other boys had been sent back to class.

She read it and nodded. "Thank you, Kieran. You'd better take yourself back to class." She paused. "It can be hard to choose friends wisely, sometimes. Maybe today has taught you something about that, because what's been happening has affected someone in your own family." She held up my page. "You've written something very honest here, Kieran. I know it will mean a lot to your cousin."

Bon was going to sleep over at our house that night. He would walk home from school alongside me and Gina. I wondered if Mrs. Gallagher had called Mom, because I was sent back to the classroom with just a warning, and without the playground-suspension punishment I found out had been given to Mason, Lucas, and a few of the others.

In the afternoon, I waited for Gina at the front school gate as I usually did. Julia wheeled her purple bike and walked with a group of girls from her class, some of the kids she had attracted since the day she'd arrived — Amy, Shona, Emma, and Amber, all laughing and chatting to one another. A short distance behind them, Bon walked in silence. On the sidewalk outside, everyone said their good-byes and set off in different directions.

I saw Julia squeeze Bon's shoulder and say, "It'll be OK."

"Yeah," Bon replied in a flat, unconvinced voice.

Julia strapped her helmet on and launched herself onto her bike. "See you," she said, looking at Bon and me in turn. "Remember everything we talked about."

She waited for us to reply *yes*, which Bon did softly, and I did nervously. "Remember," Julia said one more time before riding away. I wondered if she would go straight home to the trailer park, or meander around town the way I had noticed once or twice before.

Once I had Gina beside me, as well as a silent Bon, we set off for home. Bon and I avoided looking at each other. I tried willing myself to say *sorry*, but the word wouldn't form in my mouth. At last it came out, but in a mumbled voice I didn't intend and knew he probably hadn't heard. Gina was chatting about her day and the games she had played with her friends. It took her a while to realize Bon wasn't replying to her.

"Bon, you're not talking to me. What's the matter?"

CHAPTER

13

At first it had seemed like a dream fragment—the soft rustle of bedsheets, the quiet scratch of Velcro shoe straps—and so I didn't wake properly or turn over in bed to put a picture to the sounds. But then I thought I heard the window opening and a click as the fly screen was popped loose. Cold night air breezed into my room as Bon fidgeted with the screen until it slipped into the garden outside.

My eyes flew open and it was more real and strange than I could have imagined. The faint light that shone through the window was enough to show Bon dressed in more than pajamas, that even the silly wool hat with pom-poms was pulled down over his hair, its elf peak pointed up at an angle. There was the rustling of something being packed away and the sound of a zipper—a backpack zipper.

When Bon moved again, the lump of bag shadow was added to his own. He stopped for a moment, and

I sensed that he was going to look at me. Quickly, I closed my eyes and listened for him to move again. He didn't right away; it was as though he was thinking of something. Or was he still looking at me, deciding whether or not I was awake?

Seconds or minutes later—I wasn't sure—I opened my eyes again, sat up in bed, and stared as best I could across at his empty bed. I heard faint footsteps on the path outside.

"Where are you?" I asked, knowing that my voice was a nighttime whisper. There was no reply.

I thought quickly. Bon had his backpack. He had filled it with what could have been clothing, and he had taken it with him. I fumbled for the bedside light. This was more than Bon simply being awake and sitting up in bed, gazing through the window at the night. Bon had gone. He was there, in the night, and he had his backpack with him.

I rubbed my eyes and willed myself to wake up. *Think.*

Kicking off the blanket, I searched in frantic silence for clothes. With the open window, the bedroom had turned cold, and right over my pajamas I layered myself in long pants, a fleece top, thick socks, and sneakers. Last of all, I jammed my flame ski hat over my head and ears, all the while moving as quietly as Bon had, hoping that no one else in the house would wake. I stopped then, looking once at the closed bedroom door and at the open window. I was about to do something alone, something that my head and fast breathing told me might need an adult's help. I was about to walk out into the darkness of our town and try to find my cousin. He had packed a bag. I *had* to find him.

My feet found the ground outside the window, first the patch of garden and then the concrete of the driveway. The fastest way to search would be on my bike, and I walked softly to where it was propped in the usual place against the back wall of the carport. The other bike was not there.

How could I find him? He could have gone in any direction.

Getting my bike to the street quietly would mean carrying it, the same as I guessed Bon had just done. I heaved it up so that the top of the frame rested hard on one shoulder.

It wasn't until the end of the sidewalk that I felt safe enough to put my bike down and coast slowly toward the shopping center. Even then, the click of wheel cogs sounded too loud against the night silence of the empty road. From the distant highway came the occasional soft engine moan of a truck climbing a hill, but though I strained to listen, there was no sound of movement in any street nearby.

There was an unwelcome taste in my mouth, the flavor of feeling afraid. I swallowed hard, knowing how aimless my riding felt, and stopped to organize my thoughts. I tried to put myself into Bon's head and to think the way he might have.

I looked back in the direction of the highway, then pushed and pedaled my bike into a deliberate sort of speed. *The trailer park. Julia.* Somewhere nearby, a dog began to bark, and I swore quietly at it to stop, to not give me away. I passed the shops, the Tealeaf Café, the Travelers' Rest Motel, the park, and the turnoff to the soccer field, all the while pedaling fast and turning my head from left to right, back to where I'd been and then to where I thought it was best to head. Even with the glow of the streetlights, I was straining my eyes for the movement of another boy on a bike, and I was worrying that the direction I'd chosen was completely wrong.

I saw him then.

The glare of lights from the twenty-four-hour service station near the highway was visible now, and on the last stretch of Sheridan Street was Bon. I couldn't see his bike, but I could see his small, distant figure standing near the last streetlight. I pedaled fast. At some point, he spotted me coming, and then he was picking up the old bike, stumbling onto the seat, and cranking the pedals. I didn't dare call out.

I knew I could pedal faster than him, but as I got closer, I realized how fast he was pedaling as well. Suddenly, I could see that he was no longer shaky on a bike, that he had found his sense of balance. His confidence was unnerving and unexpected.

"Bon, stop," I said a little breathlessly as my bike caught up to his.

He didn't reply or even look at me.

"Bon, stop. You have to."

He kept riding. His feet pumped up, down, up, down, and he stared straight ahead. It was as though he knew exactly where he was going.

"Bon, listen to me. Stop."

The tires of our bikes hissed along the road. The lights of the service station loomed closer and closer, and still Bon refused to say anything.

"Please, stop." My voice had panic in it.

"Why?" he replied abruptly. "Why do I have to stop? You're not the boss of me."

"Stop pedaling."

"No!"

"Please. I don't know where you're going. You have to come back."

"What if I don't want to come back?"

"But you have to."

Abruptly, Bon squeezed the hand brakes and brought his bike to a stop, the brake pads hissing and squealing against the wheel rims. I let my bike go a little farther ahead before turning and coming to a halt in front of him. "You have to come back," I repeated.

He stared back at me, unblinking. He didn't say anything for a moment, but took his fingers away from the handlebars to pull at the straps on his backpack. "No," he said quietly.

"But you *have* to," I insisted.

"Did your parents send you after me?"

"No." There was almost a desperate laugh in the word as I said it. "I heard you leave. It's the middle of the night. It's not safe. You're by yourself and . . ." I paused for breath. "And it's freezing cold, and I don't know where you're going."

My hands were stiff and sore from the handlebars. Bon had been thorough; I saw that he had a pair of wool gloves on—*my* wool gloves, I realized. His silly hat with the furry pom-poms sat low over his face and covered all of his hair, except for his braid, which trailed out from under the wool in a blond knotted rope down his back. His helmet was strapped on over the top and it looked kind of comical, though I didn't smile about it. He turned away from me—in the direction of our town, and then at where the highway led from distant north to distant south. He looked at where the trailer park was.

"Please, come back, Bon."

He didn't reply.

"Where are you going?" I ventured.

Bon's breath trembled. "Nobody wants me here," he told me at last, without looking back. "Not really. I know *you* don't." He met my eyes. "You don't want me. You don't even like me. Julia is my only friend." Then he added softly, "And Gina. But she's only little."

It took me a few seconds to realize what he had said, and in that moment, Bon had his fingers back on the handlebars and had repositioned his left foot onto the pedal.

"You have to come home," I repeated. The last word had come out without me even thinking. *Home.*

"Why?" Bon demanded.

"Because it's not true what you said. It's not true that nobody wants you. Everyone does. Nan. My mom and dad. Gina."

"But what about you?" Bon asked. "You don't want to be friends with me. You want to be friends with kids like Mason and Lucas. And you want them to be friends with you. Except it's not working out like that."

"What do you mean?" I asked.

"You want to be popular," he said.

I didn't know what to say next. Bon fidgeted with the handlebar grips, and then he spun a pedal backward so that the bike chain rattled loudly in the silence. All I felt was cold, and I shivered a cloud of nervous breath into the space between us.

"I had a friend," I told him softly. "Before you came to visit that time. My dad's party." I looked down at the handlebars of my bike and at the dark road surface, feeling as though I were sharing my deepest secret. "Connor. But he moved away and I never saw him again."

"And you miss him," Bon stated flatly.

I nodded.

"Would you miss *me*?" he asked. "Because we're cousins and not friends?"

He looked at me carefully. I couldn't read the expression on his face and had no way of knowing what could happen next. "Yes," I answered, but felt as though this reply was carried away by the night air and the next long silence. "Please, come home, Bon. I'm sorry about what happened at school. At first I thought it might be funny, and then I knew it wouldn't be. But it was too late to make the other kids stop."

Sorry. Finally it came out clearly, the one word that

I hoped would put everything right. "I'm sorry," I told him one last time, worrying that whatever happened next would be final.

Bon began to pedal away.

He went down as far as the glow of the last streetlight reached, then turned his bike and rode slowly back past me. I felt too tired to keep wondering about where in the night Bon had intended to go. He didn't say anything on the ride home, but it was a silence I was grateful for, because perhaps it meant that I had been forgiven.

I couldn't think clearly the next day. I was tired from lack of sleep and exhausted by the thought of what had happened in the night. Bon had ridden away on my bike. He had refused to say where he had been going, and I worried that he was going to do it again.

"Late night, Kieran?" Mr. Garcia asked, because he could see I was fumbling with the schoolwork I usually completed without any problems.

"Chicken," Lucas hissed at me at the beginning of recess. "Running off to tell Julia Barrett. Might as well have been a teacher."

"So you *are* on your cousin's side now," Mason said. "Some friend you are, writing all that stuff about us for the principal to read."

I watched as the two of them walked across to the office. I had been given a lecture by Mom and Dad, but Mason, Lucas, and the others were missing recess for a week, and Mrs. Gallagher had also made them write apologies to read in person to Bon. But I knew, from the sneers they had directed at Bon on the playground already that morning, that their apologies meant just about nothing.

Nobody wants me here. It hurt to hear Bon's voice in my head, telling me exactly what I'd thought and said to him in the weeks since he had arrived in town.

I had made a point of sitting right next to him at breakfast that morning, and I willed him to look at me and say something. But at first he had spooned up mouthfuls of cereal and gazed into his bowl as though it were a mirror. I had felt invisible.

"I want to sit next to Bon!" Gina had protested when she arrived at the table.

"We can share," I'd told her. "Sit on the end chair, Gina."

"That's not next to, that's near," she had grumbled, but she'd sat down anyway.

I'd offered Bon the bottle of apple juice and he took it silently, poured a glass for himself and then one for Gina, and passed it back to me.

"Thanks, Bon," I had said.

"It's a pleasure," he'd replied in his precise voice. And then—as though he suddenly found his reply as weird and old-fashioned as it sounded—he had smiled to himself.

My shoulders drooped in relief.

Mom was over at the island fixing our lunches, already dressed in her supermarket uniform. But she stopped the cutting and wrapping to watch what had happened with us over at the table. "It looks very friendly over there," she remarked. "Have I missed the signing of a peace treaty?"

I glanced sideways at Bon. "Something like that," I answered, trying to sound cool and relaxed.

"Very good to see," she had said approvingly, and mostly to me. "I'm really pleased."

I nodded quickly, and maybe too anxiously. The picture of Bon riding away into the night was difficult to erase. That we had woken no one up was a miracle. After we had pedaled back to the corner of the street, we had lifted the bikes to our shoulders and carried them all the way to the end of our carport. We had climbed back through the open bedroom window, and I had pulled the screen back into place. We had peeled off warm clothes and climbed back into our beds. But I had stayed awake for a long time afterward, because I had nearly lost Bon and it had been my fault. I had nearly lost him, but then I brought him home.

Now, on the playground at recess, I looked for him. Of course he was with Julia and the circle of girls, just the same as every other school day. I wanted to talk to him, but he was part of whatever conversation Julia was leading. There was a soccer game happening on the back field, but I didn't have the energy to run and chase a ball. So I sat on one of the seats outside the library instead. It was the very place where Bon would sometimes sit, drawing or writing in his book.

I had told him about Connor.

I hadn't talked to anyone else about how Connor and I had been best friends for nearly two whole years, before he had simply stopped coming to school. We had played all sorts of games together. We had visited each other's homes and had sleepovers. Connor told good jokes and could draw funny, crazy pictures. His books and some of his artwork had been left behind, along with the seat where he had sat beside me in class. Miss Denny, our teacher, could only say, "Kieran, I'm sorry. It seems Connor and his family have left town. None of us knew, and I'm waiting to find out his new school so that I can send his things on. If I find out, maybe you can write to him. I know you're missing him."

It had been the year I'd turned nine. Miss Denny never had found out where Connor had gone, but she had given me some of his artwork to keep. It was still stowed away in my bedroom at home. This was the most I had let myself think about him in a very long time.

You want to be popular.

I realized that I was never going to be best friends with Lucas and Mason. There were lots of kids I liked and who I played with, but no one was quite the same as Connor. I still missed him.

"Hi, Kieran."

The voice startled me. Julia had left her group of friends and sat down on the seat next to me. "You don't usually sit here. Are you OK?"

"Yes," I replied. "Just tired."

Julia waited for more of an answer.

"I'm thinking about stuff," I admitted.

She nodded.

Bon had left the group of girls as well. He looked across to where we sat, but did not walk over. Instead, he wandered around the edges of other kids and their games.

"It's easy being part of a group," Julia said, "and it's hard to walk away and do the things you know are right. But if it's the right thing, other kids will see that. They'll come to you and be your friend. They'll like you for who you are."

I frowned. "Why are you telling me this?" I wondered if Bon had told her about riding away in the night.

"Because I've learned it," Julia said. "And I'm telling

you because of Bon. What's happened to him here has been really unfair."

My heart sank. "I tried to stop it. I told Bon I was sorry."

"I know that. But if Bon needs you again, are you ready?"

"Ready for what?"

"To be yourself. To say if something is wrong and to stand up to people. Even people you think are your friends." She added, "I don't think I'll be at this school much longer. You know that, don't you?"

I began to feel even worse, remembering the overheard conversation in Mrs. Gallagher's office.

"I don't have cousins or brothers and sisters," Julia said. "You and Bon are lucky to have each other. Maybe it's taken you a while to get that. And you've made a promise. To me, anyway. Now you have to show Bon it's a promise. OK?"

The bell rang for the end of recess and Julia stood up.

"OK," I replied.

Julia smiled. It was a warm smile that I struggled to return.

"See you, Kieran. See you again sometime."

It was the last day that Julia would be at school.

She had told her friends the same thing. *See you again sometime.*

The other girls probably thought it was a strange thing to say, but once a few days had gone by and Julia did not return to school, I could see and hear them beginning to worry.

Amy and Amber had gone down to the trailer park one day after school.

"She wasn't there," Amber said on the playground. "The people who run the place said she had left. That's all they'd tell us."

"And we couldn't believe someone like Julia would live in a place like that," Amy added.

From what the girls went on to say, I started to find out that no one had actually visited Julia at the trailer park, that she had always said things like, *No, I'll meet you in town.* She had not wanted anyone to see where she was staying.

I knew Bon was the one I needed to ask. "Where's Julia?"

He was sitting on the seats outside the school library, reading a book. His shoulders dropped at my question. "She's gone."

"Gone? But what happened? Where has she gone?"

"I don't know for sure. Not yet."

The girls marched up to Bon and asked him the same questions. "But you *must* know something," Amy told him in a demanding voice. "You and Julia were always hanging around together, and not just at school. More than *we* ever did."

And Bon replied in much the same way he had to me. Except when the girls persisted, he added angrily, "Leave me alone!" and went away into the library to avoid their questions.

I followed him. "Do you know something you're not telling?" I asked when I found him over at the fiction shelves.

He was frowning at the book spines. "I only know what I know," he answered.

I thought about this a moment, but didn't feel any less worried. "Bon? Is Julia OK?"

"Yes," he replied, his voice a mixture of sadness and certainty. "I know she's OK. Things have worked out right, the way she told me they would."

"You need to tell the other kids what you know. They need to know she's OK. Amy and Amber and all those girls are worrying. They'll start making up stories and it won't all be the truth. You have to tell them."

He sighed. "I suppose," he said. "If they want to believe *me,* that is."

But Bon didn't say anything to the other kids, and by the end of the week, stories were being told at school. That the police had visited the trailer park. That someone had seen Julia's mom driven away in the back of the local patrol car. That Julia and a man had walked out of the police station together, and that was the last time Julia had been seen in town.

On the playground, Julia's friends worried and speculated until Mrs. Gallagher came over from her office and explained a little of what had really happened. Both fifth-grade classes sat on the carpet in my classroom, and Mrs. Gallagher—who always stood to speak when it was the whole school—borrowed Mr. Garcia's chair and sat down.

"Julia is fine," she began. "I need to start by reassuring you all about that. Unpleasant things can happen in families, as some of you might know and understand only too well. Ignore any rumors that might be flying around town—Julia *is* safe and with her family. She was only with us a short while, but she was a very good member of our school community." Mrs. Gallagher paused. "I've almost lost count of the number of children who have come to our school for only a short amount of time, but let me tell you, I won't be forgetting Julia and her ideas and her generosity toward others." At this point, I saw Mrs. Gallagher look over to where Bon was sitting. "If you were friends with her, I know that you will be missing her."

I looked around the classroom and saw lots of things: Lucas and Mason and a few of the boys yawning and acting bored, Amy and a few of the girls looking lost and sad, Amber Hodges looking cranky. Other kids were gazing intently at Mrs. Gallagher and hanging on her every word, which made me wonder if some of these were the kids Nan talked about, the ones who had unhappy family lives.

And last of all there was Bon, who sat on the floor staring at his feet, trapped in his own air bubble. Bon, who I knew missed his friend probably more than anyone else in the room.

Back at the village, Julia the Fair was preparing for her own journey.

I saw Bon frown then, and it was as though Mrs. Gallagher hadn't said everything he needed to hear. Something was not finished, and still not right.

At the very end of the day, as we waited at the school gate for Gina, he abruptly said, "Julia told me to look in my bag."

"What?" I asked, not understanding at all.

"My bag," he answered. "It was one of the last things she said the other afternoon, before she left. *Look in your bag.*"

"And?" My head was still full of Julia not being around. *See you again sometime.*

Bon had an envelope in his hand. He pulled out a folded piece of paper and held it, floating, in front of me. "I found this in my bag," he said.

"What is it?"

He dropped it lower, unfolded it carefully. "I need you to read it," he said, and then looked steadily at me. "I need your help."

"Why?"

"It's from Julia. Please, you have to read it."

Kids swarmed past us, some heading off along the sidewalk, others stepping onto the buses that would take them out of town to the farms and homes I was jealous of. I took the folded note, spread it open, and read.

Dear Bon,

It was a girl's writing, upright, curled, and neat. The *g*'s, *e*'s, and *a*'s looped in a rhythm my own writing had never managed without a great deal of effort.

The ink was the color of peppermint ice cream.

I will not forget how I met you. Bad luck became good luck. I learned how to be patient and how to be brave, and now things will be safe and normal again. You have been my best friend and I want to give you the purple bike. I will not need it anymore. Things are going to happen quickly, but I will leave it for you. Show this letter to people so they know the bike is yours to keep. Until we meet again—Julia.

"But she doesn't say exactly where the bike is," Bon explained. "And I don't know what to do."

I didn't know where to begin either. Finally, I said, "I'll ask Dad."

"No," Bon replied.

It was strange—he sounded a little scared, and I wondered about that. So I threw my hands up, exasperated, and asked, "What, then?"

Bon shrugged.

"It'll be at the trailer park," I reasoned. "Or maybe even at the police station. Dad can help us."

I could tell that Bon wasn't convinced. "Can you think of a better idea?" I was quiet for a moment. "That man," I said then. "Someone saw Julia leave the police station with a man. Do you know who he was?"

"It was her dad," Bon replied. "He'd been looking for her. Julia was a missing person, and now she is *found.*"

Bon turned away when I sat down beside him at morning recess. He was drawing in his book, and I tried to make it obvious that I wasn't trying to peek at whatever picture he was working on. Instead, I looked out at the playground and said, "Hi," as though I came to sit here every other day.

"Hello," he answered vaguely.

Little and big kids shouted and played around us. It was, I thought, a little like being on a remote island, the seat where we were sitting. I felt distant from the noise and movement on the playground. I could see the boys from my class chasing a ball around. Mason and Lucas ran alongside each other, calling and gesturing to each other, favoring each other whenever the ball had to be passed. It was as though they were a team within a team. A team I was no longer part of. Bon's seat on the playground had become my seat as well.

I could hear the rapid scratching of his pen as he drew. Suddenly, it reminded me of the soft noises that had come to me in the darkness of my bedroom before Bon had disappeared into the night. Even now, days later, I swallowed hard at the memory of it, flinching at the pictures in my head—Bon and his wool hat, his backpack, *my* bike, pedaling out toward the highway with the night traffic of semis roaring past him. It was a troubling darkness I couldn't shake off, where I tossed and turned to the rhythm of Bon riding away from us.

"I still can't believe you did that," I told him, the thought tumbling out in a rush.

"What?"

"The way you snuck out that night. It was freezing cold, and dark. You were out there by yourself."

He looked at me then. "I've been out at night before."

"By yourself?"

"Yes. When I was at the trailer park, and then at the hotel. I went walking."

"How many times?"

"A few."

"But *why?*"

"Just to look around. To see what happened in town at night."

I stared at him. "Weren't you scared?"

"A bit. But it was like a challenge."

"What do you mean?"

"I used to be scared of the dark. I thought I could hear noises and voices all the time. I got sick of being frightened, so I made myself go out into it—the dark." Then he said softly, "But only when my mom had remembered to take her medication and was able to sleep. Then I could get away."

I thought about this. "But where were you going on the bike the other night?"

Bon took a while to answer. "I don't know. Not really. I wasn't sure I wanted to come back."

His reply made me flinch and want to say *sorry* yet again. Instead, I asked, "But the nights you went out walking, where did you go? What did you see?"

He laid the pen against the page of his drawing and closed his book over it. "The people in the bakery, they work at night. Their lights were on and I could see them through the shop window; I could hear a bit of what they were saying. Some house lights were on, and I could hear televisions playing different shows and movies. And some teenagers were sitting under that really old bridge. I heard them talking and laughing together. I could hear cans being opened and bottles clinking, and there was cigarette smoke. One time, someone else was out walking really late at night, and I think he saw me. But I hid, and it was OK."

I sensed that Bon was enjoying my surprise.

"So it *was* like a challenge. And I met the challenge." Then worry crossed his face. "Are you going to tell on me now?"

"No." I paused. "But would you do it again if I came with you? We could take the bikes."

He looked at me a little suspiciously. "Maybe," Bon mumbled, and I could hear his voice closing down a little. "But why?"

I wondered why I had even thought to suggest the idea. It was like nothing I had ever thought or dared to do, but suddenly I wanted to see things the way Bon did. I wanted to understand his thoughts, and I wanted to understand Bon.

That night, in the darkness between Friday and Saturday, the rain woke me, but somehow not Bon. For ages, I lay listening to the clatter of water on the roof while he slept, his shape totally motionless under the blanket. And suddenly, I had been asleep, and he was awake, dressed, and kneeling beside my bed.

"Kieran." Close to my ear, he whispered my name. *"Are you ready?"* His breath had a faint smell of toothpaste, and when I turned to look at him, he put a finger to his lips. He had a small flashlight in his other hand, which, just once, he flicked on and off. I almost wished

I hadn't made the suggestion, but the challenge teased at me. We didn't talk the whole time that we climbed out through the bedroom window, found our bikes, and carried them up the driveway. Not until we were some way down the street did we begin whispering.

"I know which places have dogs that bark," Bon told me, something I could easily have told *him*.

I felt cold and nervously excited. I had strained to listen for any other movement in the house as I'd dressed, and I would have jumped straight back into bed at the first sound of Mom or Dad awake.

We launched ourselves onto the bikes and pedaled silently along the middle of our avenue, keeping our wheels away from crunching gravel. My watch told me it was a bit after two o'clock. A haze of fog was in the air and my breath came out in cloudy puffs. All the houses I could see had darkened windows and only the soft moon glow to show gardens, fences, and cars parked in driveways or on front lawns. But farther down the hill was the central part of town, bathed in a golden glow of streetlights. Everything was utterly still and quiet, but my heart was pumping quickly. Bon looked from left to right; he looked behind, to where we had come from. He was watchful and cautious.

We rode in shadow until we reached the edge of the main street shops.

"Now what?" I asked.

"Listen," Bon instructed.

I could hear murmuring voices and small bursts of laughter coming from the direction of the bridge.

"Duane and Annie and Mitch, Melanie, and Rob. I think that's all the names I've heard from there," Bon said. "Each time I've been out, I've heard them sitting there under the bridge. It's like their secret meeting place."

I heard the clink of a bottle and saw a faint drift of cigarette smoke.

"We should keep moving," I said.

"There's somewhere we need to go to next," Bon whispered, and pedaled his bike ahead. It was the Imperial Hotel that we stopped at. Not at the main entrance, but at the plain side door marked GUEST ROOMS. Bon fumbled in a pocket and suddenly had a key in his hand. He unlocked and opened the door as confidently as I might have opened our front door at home. We pulled our bikes inside the entrance, away from the streetlight glow.

"Wouldn't someone else be staying in that room?" I whispered in alarm.

Bon shrugged, then suddenly hissed, "Car!" We tumbled inside as the engine sound came closer. The bikes were a nuisance at this moment, and we clunked and bumped them awkwardly through the doorway. Bon had pushed the door quickly and quietly shut, and now we stood in total gloom. The car drove past along the main street, then made a turn somewhere nearby and began to fade a little from our hearing.

"What now?"

"There's stairs," he whispered, setting his bike against the wall. "Follow me."

It was nearly impossible to see him, and I put a hand on his shoulder so as not to lose him. I could hear his hands reach out and find the walls with his fingertips, his nails making a soft tapping sound until he got his bearings. He began to walk, and I followed. The steps were carpeted and smelled musty. We reached a landing and climbed a last short stretch of steps before stopping at another door. I heard Bon's key in another lock, and the door opened.

My family and I had never visited Bon and his mom here. A streetlight shone in through the only window and showed a small room. There were two beds, a wardrobe, a sink and mirror, and a bedside table with a digital clock that blinked the wrong time, over and over. I could smell musty carpet and something else, a lingering sweetness of wine or beer. It felt creepy, and I almost expected someone to sit up in one of the beds, stare at us, and scream.

"No one else is staying here," Bon said, raising his voice beyond a whisper. "But don't turn the light on," he warned, walking over to the window.

"How come you've got a key?" I asked. My voice was shaky, and I could feel the goose bumps on my arms and legs.

"Mom gave her key back to the hotel manager," Bon said, "but I'd already had another key cut."

"Why?'

"Because my mom would lose things," he answered. "Especially things like keys."

I walked over to the window as well. "You can see everything from here," I said. "The whole town, and all the way to the highway. Even the old railroad bridge. It looks like a black skeleton."

"Yes," Bon agreed. "I like this view. I used to stand here sometimes at night and look at everything. In the daytime as well. I drew pictures of the town and the way everything looked." After a pause, he added, "I even thought maybe Mom and I were going to live here for good. It was better than lots of other places we'd stayed. And way better than staying at the trailer park."

"Like Julia had to?"

"Yes," he answered softly.

There was something I had to ask. "Did you know

Julia before you started school here? Because it was like you did. Like you were already friends."

"How could you tell?"

I thought quickly of the first moment I had seen Bon and Julia together, and then of everything Julia had told me about Bon. And about myself.

"It was as though you knew lots about each other."

I heard him let out a long sigh that seemed to mean, *OK, I'll tell you now.*

"Mom told me she was taking me up to Nan's. We left the last place we were staying and drove for hours. Then our car needed gas. We came to one of those big highway service centers." He paused. "And Julia was there with her mom. Their car had broken down; there was oil on the ground *everywhere*. Her mom was really worked up and asked my mom where we were going. She offered us money to bring them along as well. So that's what happened."

It took me a moment to think all this through, to add it to what little I had known to start with.

Beside me in the darkness, Bon fidgeted with the blind cord. Then he said, "Her mom sat in the front with my mom, and they spent the trip talking about all sorts of stuff. Julia's mom was really nervous, as though someone were after them." He paused again.

"I didn't like her. She made the inside of our car feel *really* weird. And Julia was so quiet at first; she stared out her window and didn't say anything. My mom put some music on, *loud,* and she and Julia's mom kept talking. They smoked just about a whole packet of cigarettes, too. That was when Julia started talking with me, and the rest of the way to the trailer park, we whispered little bits and pieces about ourselves to each other. It was harder at the trailer park, because Julia's mom wouldn't let us be together much. She told Julia not to tell me anything, but it was too late by then."

Bon let out a long breath, as though he had just run a race.

"How come you and your mom left the trailer park?"

"My mom wound up thinking Julia's mom was a bit weird, too. I didn't tell her what I knew, but Mom thought there was something strange going on, and she didn't want to hang around to find out what, exactly. So we came here. It was quieter than the trailer park. Mom slept a lot. I wrote and drew. I read stories." He glanced at me. "I met up with Julia sometimes."

"And you had free breakfasts at the café," I reminded him.

"It gets hard for my mom to plan things each day," Bon said in a resigned voice. "It was easier if I just did the things I needed to do, like breakfast and stuff. I was used to it. I was OK. I *can* look after myself, you know. I don't need grown-ups."

Yes, you do, I thought, then remarked out loud, "This feels creepy," because again I was gripped by the thought that someone else could be lurking in the darkness of the small room or the hallway outside. "Bon, can we go now?"

"You haven't asked me the next question," he replied.

"The next question?"

"Yes," he said, and there was the hint of a laugh in his voice. "About who might be after Julia's mom."

By now I knew. "Julia's dad."

"Yes."

"Why?"

"Because Julia wasn't supposed to be with her mom. She was supposed to be with her dad, but her mom had *stolen* her. And she'd been hiding Julia for two years." Unexpectedly, Bon's hand rested on my shoulder. "And now Julia is back with her dad." His voice dropped. "Except I don't know where they've gone. That's still the hard part."

We both fell silent, and the darkness and emptiness of the room started to swallow us again.

"Bon, I think we should go now." He stayed at the window a while longer, so I said it again, adding, "Please. I don't really like it here."

"It's OK," he answered without looking at me. "It's just an empty room. *My* empty room." But at last, we were outside again, the door locked, and the two of us going downstairs, with me gripping the back of Bon's sweatshirt. And then we were outside with our bikes in the chilly air.

"You *are* scared, aren't you?" Bon said. "It's OK, you know."

"I just want to go home," I admitted. "It really feels weird being out by ourselves like this."

I looked around nervously, expecting to see house lights being turned on, or the local police patrol car turning silently onto the street, its lights blindingly bright. I suddenly longed to be back at home and said urgently, "Bon, we have to go. *Now.*"

We pedaled quickly and in silence. Soon enough, we had left the shops and the main street behind. I was starting to feel tired.

But as we reached the corner and started back onto our street, my heart jumped. "Oh, no," I whispered.

I knew Dad would be furious. We could see him in the front yard. He was turning his head in frantic half circles, and when he spotted us, I could see the way his shoulders dropped and his arms folded themselves across his chest.

His voice was a controlled, soft growl. "What on *earth* do you two think you're doing?"

Bon stared at Dad. His mouth was open and I could tell he was frightened.

"Just riding," I said, shocked that we'd been caught.

"Just riding," Dad repeated. "At three in the morning?" He jabbed a thumb toward the house. "Inside, *now.* By the front door, please, not the window."

My hands were clenched tight to the handlebars, and I could see Bon's were as well.

Dad pointed. "Just put the bikes down; I'll put them away. Go inside and get back into bed, both of you. We'll talk about this in the morning."

As I followed Bon to the door, I heard Dad mutter, *"Just riding.* Well, there won't be any of *that* for a while."

We were in a lot of trouble.

My parents sat Bon and me down the next morning before we'd even begun breakfast. I knew how my parents' faces would be—Dad frowning and plain mad, and Mom with an expression somewhere between cranky and upset.

"Look at me when I'm speaking to you," Dad instructed.

But I shook my head. I was at the edge of the living room sofa, staring hard at the carpet and feeling as though I wanted to launch myself out of the room and through the back door.

Bon, meanwhile, had squashed himself as far back into the sofa as he could.

"What," Dad went on, "was going on in your heads? What were you doing out on the streets at three in the morning?"

I thought hard about how to answer. "I was teaching Bon to ride." I knew it sounded like a lie.

"What?" Dad exclaimed.

I looked up. "I was teaching Bon how to ride the bike. There's no traffic early in the morning, so it was safer." Which sounded even more pathetic.

Dad and Mom exchanged openmouthed looks, shaking their heads at the same time.

"Kieran," Mom said, "you'll have to do a lot better than that. Bon? What have you got to say?"

"I needed the practice," Bon answered.

"You needed the practice," Dad repeated.

Bon quickly added, "I'd never ridden a bike till I came here. Kieran was helping me."

"At three in the morning?" Mom and Dad chorused.

"Yes," Bon replied in the precise voice I hadn't heard in a while. "Like Kieran said, we decided there was less traffic and it was safer."

Of course it wasn't enough to convince my parents.

"Is Kieran in trouble?" Gina asked as she made her morning entrance, complete with pink pony pajamas and a handful of dolls. Then she looked at Bon. "Is Bon in trouble, *too*?" she asked in a more alarmed voice.

We were grounded, my parents decided. No outings—and no bikes. Bon and I were banned from riding anywhere for two weeks.

"And you will be driven to and from school," Mom told us, shaking her head. "Honestly, you two . . ."

Lost for words, she had Bon pack up his things and drove him back to Nan's. I stayed on the couch for a long time afterward. I didn't feel hungry enough to eat breakfast, and my head was full of how boring the next two weeks were going to be.

I had never practiced so many soccer skills in my entire life. Each afternoon, I worked my way around the entire backyard, from the driveway gate to Dad's shed and along the back fence to the clothesline. I dribbled the ball at a walk and a sprint, I worked on the foot flicks that sent the ball up in the air to be caught and balanced on my forehead. I was determined not to be a reserve-list player for another year. I really wanted Mr. Garcia to see how much I'd improved and how ready I was for the next soccer season. I counted the days grounded so far—one, two, three—and then added up what was left.

But when I daydreamed too much, the ball went astray. A few times, it even went over the back fence and I had to climb through the wire to retrieve it, stealing extra minutes just to be on the wrong side of the fence. I wished that I could go somewhere—a park, shopping, a friend's house. Friends? I guessed that

Mason and Lucas had crossed me off their list by now. In my head, I ran through all the other names of kids that I knew, picturing their houses and their parents. I paused at the end of the list, kicking the ball back into our yard before Mom noticed I was outside the boundary. *Bon.* That was the name I came to last. And I realized that, without ever intending to, I had come to know him best of anybody.

Mom and Dad didn't say very much to me for the first couple of days. I wasn't used to punishments with groundings and long silences, and I was glad to get to school each day, even if it meant being driven there, as though I were five years old.

"Why aren't we walking?" Gina asked.

"Because," Mom answered, "your brother hasn't been responsible enough."

"Stop looking at me, Gina," I muttered, because my sister's wide-eyed look was making me feel as though I were someone who should be doing time in jail. After a couple of days, Mom began to ask the sorts of questions that I'd been dreading.

"What were you thinking, Kieran? Didn't it occur to you that we'd find out? That we'd be beside ourselves with worry if you hadn't returned?" And finally, a question I was only a little comfortable replying to: "Where did you go?"

"Just around the main part of town. The shops, the park, the streets nearby. That's all," I said.

My answer didn't make Mom any happier, and she gave me the kind of look that seemed to say, *There's more that you're not telling me.*

Nan dropped Bon at our place the following Friday for his weekend sleepover. "Could be a long weekend for boys who suddenly seem to like being out on their bikes together," Nan remarked at the door.

"A *very* long weekend," Mom agreed, then added, "What's that?" as Nan held something up in one hand.

"A door key." Nan glanced sideways at Bon, who I could see had been hoping to slip through the front door and avoid any unwelcome conversations.

He heaved a loud sigh. "A key to the hotel room Mom and I had. I wanted to go back and visit it sometimes. And I showed Kieran as well."

Mom exchanged a look with Nan that I couldn't read. And then glared at me.

"The hotel is not your home anymore, Bon," Nan told him. "Or the trailer park. You and I have had that talk." She said to Mom, "I'm returning it to the Imperial this morning, just to avoid any more trouble."

"We've got one more week of being grounded, and then everything is back to normal," Bon reminded her.

"Normal!" Nan laughed and kissed him on the forehead. I wondered why the word amused her so much. "*Normal* is something we're still working on, my dear."

Being stuck at home felt anything but normal, but having Bon around felt different now. Instead of avoiding him, I found myself sharing the house and the backyard with him. He wasn't really interested in kicking a ball around, and he still spent time playing with Gina. But as Friday became Saturday, and morning drifted into afternoon, we found ourselves together at the computer being game opponents and, later, sprawled on the living room floor watching a movie. We agreed on pizza as our Saturday takeout dinner treat when Mom asked us to choose, and we finished the day quietly in our room. Bon lay on the trundle bed, drawing in his book. I began to read a magazine, but wasn't concentrating very well.

"Have you got that note with you?" I asked him.

He nodded, pointing at his backpack on the floor. "It's in there. Why?"

I rolled over on my bed and looked at him. "Because I'm going to ask Dad if he can help."

"But your dad's mad at us. We're in trouble."

"It won't be forever, and the note is proof that you're supposed to have Julia's bike now. So whoever's got it has to hand it over. Dad will make them," I reassured him.

We stared at each other a moment, before Bon shrugged his shoulders and picked up his drawing pen.

"What is it?" I asked.

"Nothing," he mumbled.

I realized then. "Bon, Dad's not a scary guy. Are you frightened of him?"

"No," Bon replied, in a voice that clearly meant *yes*.

"Dad knows lots of people around town. The guys on his team—there's a high-school teacher, a couple of truckers, a mechanic, guys who work on farms. He knows the people who run the trailer park. And Jacko, the goalie, he's a police officer. If we show Dad the note, he'll be able to help out. You'll see." I waited for Bon to look up. "OK?"

Bon gazed at his artwork in silence before reaching for the backpack and pulling out Julia's note. "Here," he said, and held it out for me to take. "But don't let your dad keep it. I want it back."

"Sure," I agreed, and stood up to put it in the top drawer of my desk.

The right time to ask had to be the following morning, and I waited for the familiar quiet sounds of Dad preparing for his morning run. Quickly, I threw on clothes and sneakers, tucking the note into the button-down back pocket of my shorts.

Dad was raiding the fridge for fruit juice.

"Can I come for a run, or am I grounded from that as well?" I asked.

He took a swig straight from the juice bottle, something I had always been told *not* to do, and looked me up and down. "No," he answered with a long sigh. "Come on."

It was wet outside. The rain misted onto my face and head, cool and delicate. At first, I stayed behind Dad, following the slight stamp marks his running shoes left on the wet grass that ran along the roadside. It occurred to me that I'd been doing the morning run like this for a long time, always following behind him, always struggling to keep up, and knowing not to talk at the wrong moments, not to disturb Dad's focus and concentration. I'd ask him once we'd stopped at the park.

With effort, I increased my speed and moved alongside him, surprised that I had managed it. I kept beside him all the way along Hanley Street and left onto Otway Road, until we came to the park at the next corner. We were both soaked from the misting rain, and instead of stopping on the wet grass, we jogged across to one of the picnic shelters. Using the bench seats, Dad put himself through his usual leg stretches, before rotating his arms and shoulders, heaving several loud, slow puffs, and sitting down. I sat down on the bench opposite, feeling tired but pleased as well.

"You kept up well," he told me. "You getting a bit fitter these days?"

"I guess."

"Maybe it was all the bike riding. That and the night air."

I looked away guiltily.

"It was a dumb thing to do," he continued, "but you know that by now."

I sighed. "Yeah, I know."

"But you've kept up today," Dad repeated, looking pleased. "You paced yourself well, nice even breathing—what's happened?"

"I just wanted to . . . get better at stuff," I answered. "I don't want to be on the soccer reserve list for another season."

Dad nodded. Across on Sheridan Street, the streetlights blinked off in the first glow of morning, and the familiar elderly dog walkers made their way along the sidewalk toward the convenience store. I could hear the rain hitting the roof more loudly.

"It's good to hear you sound so determined," Dad replied at last. "You've got the makings of a good team player, Kieran. Keep trying and don't lose heart." He paused and took a deep, thoughtful breath. "Personally, I don't know how many seasons I've got left in me."

I felt a little alarmed. "What do you mean?"

Dad tapped his knees. "I'm one of the oldest guys on the team. Things hurt for a lot longer after a game than they used to. I don't feel like ruining my health by playing a tough game for longer than I should, against players who are younger, fitter, and faster." He laughed. "Don't look so worried. I'll still do the morning run, and maybe I'll look at getting into coaching instead. You've set yourself a challenge, Kieran, but you don't have to try to be me, you know. I'm just a guy who kicks a ball around with a bunch of friends. I'm no star. I just try to keep fit and enjoy myself. Do you understand?"

I shrugged. "I guess."

"Come running with me for the fun of it. If you make it onto the starting team next year, I'll be happy. If you're a reserve, I'll be happy. If you keep trying, I'll be happy. OK?"

I nodded. "I guess."

"Well, then — ready for the run home?"

"Almost," I mumbled, looking down and trying to rehearse what had to be said.

"What is it?"

"Dad," I said with an effort. "I need your help."

"My help? You got homework overdue?"

"No . . ." My voice drifted away as I fumbled in my back pocket. "It's not help for me, really. It's for Bon." I held the envelope out. "There's a letter inside to

Bon," I explained. "From a friend. Except Bon doesn't really know what to do, and I thought you might."

"You've become a bit of a team, you two," Dad said. "Who's the friend?"

"Julia. She was a new girl at school—for a while." I paused. "She doesn't live here anymore. Her dad found her and took her home again."

Dad nodded. "I've heard the talk around town. About the mother being on the run with the daughter. That the girl was a missing person. And two years later, the father finds her again—here in town! She and Bon were friends?"

"I think she was his best friend."

Dad gently unfolded the piece of paper. Then his lips moved silently as he read. "Well, isn't this something," he said at last. "*Till we meet again.* That's a nice ending. So Bon has inherited her bike. He'll have to keep practicing his bike-riding skills, now, won't he?"

"He has been already," I said.

"The night you two were out and about?"

"No. There was another time."

"When?" Dad leaned across the picnic table, folding his arms and bringing his face close to mine.

My voice wouldn't work properly, and the words ran together in a jumbled panic. "It was Bon. He went away one night and I followed him."

"Where to? That hotel room he had the key to?"

"No. Dad . . ."

"Tell me, Kieran. I need to hear it. *Now.*"

"Dad, I think he was running away. I went after him to make him come back."

I watched my dad close his eyes a moment, mouth a couple of words that looked like *Oh, God,* and then look back at me. "That boy," he said. "What was he thinking?"

"He thought we didn't want him."

"Was he going off after his mother?"

I shook my head. "No, I don't think so. I don't think he really knew. And he didn't want to ask you to help with the note. I think he's a little scared of you, Dad."

"Scared of me—why?"

I shrugged. "I don't know."

Dad rolled his eyes and asked, "So, that night, how did you make him come home?"

"By telling him we'd miss him. By saying that he was part of our family." I took a deep breath. "By saying sorry."

Dad fell silent for a few minutes. He sighed and looked into the distance behind me, and I guessed that he was thinking about Bon, and maybe everything that had happened in our family over the last few months. About the way Bon had changed things.

"He hasn't had an easy life," Dad said. "Your nan taking him on was the best thing. We'll be good for him in all sorts of ways. And he's going to be here with us for a long time to come. For as long as he's at school, I think."

I was surprised at how gentle my dad's voice had become. It wasn't the voice I heard at soccer practice or at games, and it wasn't even the voice I heard at our house or down in the Guys' Room, at the bottom of our backyard.

"Everyone deserves to be wanted," Dad said. "You shouldn't have been out by yourself, but you did well that night. You did really well bringing Bon home to us." He held the note up. "As for this . . . I'll track Bon's bike down for him. And I'll talk to him as well. Does he really think I'm a scary guy?" That last sentence almost had a laugh in it. "I'll have to set him straight about *that*. Funny boy."

Dad stood up and pointed a thumb in the vague direction of home. We set off across the park toward Sheridan Street, our feet splashing on the wet ground. We said nothing more, but that felt quite OK to me. I knew we'd said enough important things to each other for one morning, and I easily kept up with Dad the entire way home.

I wasn't sure who it was that realized the people down on Hammond Road were a film crew. They'd driven their van a little way and then parked on the dusty shoulder of road that made its weedy way along the outside of the school fence. They were beyond the farthest side of the playground, the spot where the odd soccer ball got kicked from time to time. On the opposite side of Hammond Road was the local cemetery, so it wasn't unusual for cars to be there. If we were outside playing, we usually took no notice.

Until today, when one of the boys shouted, "Hey! They've got a camera. They're going to film us."

The van had a large TV-station logo along its sides, and several people had climbed out and were taking in a view of the school and of everyone in the back playground. There was a woman with a microphone that she clipped onto a long pole, a man who unpacked and settled a camera onto his shoulder, and another man in a shirt and tie. He stopped to check his hair in the car's rearview mirror before walking up to the playground fence. I thought I recognized him from a weekly television news show. Mike Somebody. So must have a lot of other kids, because soccer and chasing games were quickly forgotten as we all turned and ran toward the fence, where our unusual visitors stood waiting and smiling.

"Hi, kids," said Television Mike, beaming. "We're here to ask about your friend. Julia Barrett."

My mouth dropped open in surprise, and I looked around at the gathering group of kids. More of them were still running toward us, as though the camera and microphone were magnets. And in the distance, at the very edge of the big back field near the classrooms, was Mrs. Barnes, the Thursday playground-duty teacher. She looked across and began walking quickly toward us.

Everyone began talking and shouting at once.

"Julia!" Her name began to be said over and over. Suddenly, everyone seemed to have been Julia's friend.

Mason Cutler's voice rose above everyone else's. "Yeah, man," he said in a tough, cool-guy voice. "She's been taken. Abducted by aliens."

Television Mike tried again. "Any of her best friends

195

here? Anybody know about her mom or her home life?"

I noticed the camera wasn't being pointed at our faces. It seemed to be hovering toward our legs and feet. It was only that and the sound of everybody's voices that would make it onto television, but some of the kids didn't seem to notice. They were busy trying to be famous, and everyone seemed to know something about Julia.

"She was the most popular girl in the class. Everyone liked her."

"She had good ideas about things."

"She was kind to everyone."

I listened to their voices and looked at their faces— all the girls who used to fight among themselves and then had suddenly all learned to get along well with Julia around. They had been a little lost without her.

"She never really told us where she came from."

"Julia never had friends over to visit."

"I wouldn't invite friends to visit me in a trailer park."

"Her mom was kind of scary, too."

"Yeah, really unfriendly. We know why, now."

"Julia never talked about her dad."

Everyone was competing for the camera's attention, and the comments began to change.

"If she'd been a *real* friend, she would have said

something," someone said, and there was a chorus of agreement.

I heard Lucas say, "Julia thought she was better than all of us. We could tell."

Then everyone began talking over one another. My mouth dropped open, surprised at hearing these things. I was stuck for something to say that would turn the conversation back to its starting point—about how everyone was missing Julia being here at school. Or were they?

Suddenly, Bon was somewhere nearby. I heard his voice before I actually saw him.

"It's not true!" he shouted, pushing and elbowing his way through everyone. "Nobody is saying the right thing."

Kids looked at him, surprised and annoyed by the distraction.

Mason kept up his cool-guy routine. "Just ignore him, man," he said to the camera. "The rest of us do."

Bon glared at the television crew. "Everyone is wrong. Julia knew how to be friends with people. She was a nice person—"

Abruptly, Mason snatched something from Bon's hand. It was his book of maps and inventions, and Mason held it away from Bon's panicked reach. "She was a *niiiice* person," he mimicked back at Bon.

Then Mrs. Barnes reached us.

"Turn off that camera," she called, in the same bossy voice she would have used to someone misbehaving on the playground. "Stop filming these children."

"We're not on school grounds. And we're not filming their faces," Television Mike pointed out. "It's strictly feet and voices only. We aren't standing on school premises out here."

"I don't care," Mrs. Barnes scolded. "Turn your camera off *now*." She glared at us kids. "And you children are to leave this part of the playground. All of you, up to the main quadrangle."

There was a lot of groaning, and whining voices saying, "Why, ma'am?" A couple of kids continued to make faces and give peace signs to the camera, until Mrs. Barnes threatened lunchtime detentions. "You should have spoken with our principal first," I heard her growl at the television crew.

I tried to spot Bon in the tumble of kids walking or jogging back across the field. And at the front of the group, I could see Mason. He flung a piece of paper into the air behind him, then another, as Bon jumped around him, caught between trying to retrieve his book and to pick up the pages that were now fluttering to the ground.

I ran, faster than I ever had before, right up to Mason.

In one quick move, I snatched the book from his grasp and gave him a push that sent him off-balance.

It was like looking into the eyes of a stranger. Not the Mason who had visited my house and who I would have invited away on a family vacation, but somebody I hadn't ever met and wouldn't have liked knowing. I could tell he was shocked at my pushing him, but he fought back with an equal push. Bon's book remained tightly in my grasp, and I struggled a little to keep my eyes set on Mason's face. There was a small moment where his eyes blinked in disbelief, and a tiny silence, broken by him sneering, "You're weak. Just like your girly cousin."

"And you're a bully," I managed to reply. "Leave Bon alone."

Mason walked away, a group of boys from our class falling into step with him.

"Hurry up, children!" Mrs. Barnes called from behind us. When I turned to look, it seemed as though she were standing guard against invading forces. Some of the television crew had walked back to their van, but I could see the camera now being aimed at Television Mike, and I could hear the vague sound of his voice in the distance.

Bon had gathered up his torn pages and reached out for his precious book.

I didn't hand it over. "I can help you fix it," I reassured him.

"How?" he demanded. I could hear leftover anger in his voice that minutes before had shouted, *Nobody is saying the right thing.*

"There'll be good tape in the library for fixing book pages," I told him. "Ms. Tabor won't mind us borrowing it."

His shoulders were heaving, and I saw that one hand was clenched into a fist. I put my own hand on his shoulder. "Bon, it's OK now. I can help you."

He let me carry his book and, at a table in the library, watched as I carefully, steadily reattached the pages. They were pages full of the things I had become used to — diagrams, scribbled writing, something that could have been a treasure map. And the last one that I reattached was a busy, chaotic battle scene where horses collided and swords were raised. *Our resolve was tested by the opponents of good.*

I read this messy scrawl of writing several times before looking sideways at Bon.

"This is about us," I said. "It's not Kieran the Brave or Bon the Crusader. It's us right now, and everything that's happening. Everything here at school."

Bon wiped a hand across his face. "They were talking

trash about Julia. They didn't really know her. *I* knew her better than anyone."

I didn't reply.

"I know Julia told you that you should look after me. But you don't have to, you know." Bon pointed at the library window with the end of his pen. "You should be out there." He took his book, turned past the damaged pages, and stared at a fresh, blank space. "You should be with your friends."

I looked in the direction his finger had waved, and, through the library window, I saw Mason, Lucas, Brendan, Ethan — most of the boys from my class — as they played and called to one another in the quadrangle outside. They were passing a ball between them, flicking it from hand to hand, laughing and joking around. I saw Mason turn and seem to glance in our direction, then make a comment that the others seemed to agree with: something to do with Bon and me.

I sighed. There were probably a lot of words that would be left unsaid, things to do with Mason and Lucas and their best friends, which I knew didn't include me.

"No," I told Bon. "It's OK. I don't know who my friends are, really."

"You pushed Mason," Bon said. "I saw that."

"Yes. I had to. He deserved it," I replied wearily.

"And you rescued my book. Thank you."

I watched as Bon's picture became a landscape, a hillside of tall and mysterious trees. On the horizon lay a craggy mountain range, and in between, the rooftops of houses, the spire of a church, traces of chimney smoke. It almost could have been a view of our town, the view I remembered from the window of the hotel room where Bon and his mom had stayed. Except the drawing had a trace of fantasy or fairy tale: the houses looked centuries older, and the landscape looked creepier than the fields and hills that surrounded our town. I could almost forget I was here in the school library, that there were kids all around the place reading, talking, playing board games. That Ms. Tabor was over at her desk unloading a box of new books and talking with a couple of little kids.

Thinking about the television crew disrupted my little daydream. "Bon," I said, "why didn't Julia tell someone? About her mom taking her and hiding her from her dad?"

Bon's pen stopped at the end of a curved line of black ink. He stared hard at his picture and then at me before resuming his drawing.

"Why were you the first person she told?" I asked.

"Julia was scared of her mom. *I* was scared of her

mom when she got into our car that day." Bon lifted his pen away from the page. "Julia said to me later that on the day her mom took her, everything seemed all planned out, because suddenly her mom had a different hairstyle and a different car. She had Julia's hair cut differently, too. There was another name on the documents Julia saw once or twice; someone else's address. Julia's last name got changed."

"So she was never Julia Barrett?" My voice was close to a whisper.

"No," Bon replied quietly, resuming his drawing, his mouth curved in a small smile. "She was Julia *Mitchell.*"

It took me a moment to absorb the sound of a different name. "Julia told you all of this?"

"Yes. It started when we gave them a lift. It was the first thing Julia said to me. *So who are you guys running away from?* She whispered that to me in the backseat, once our moms had started talking, because she could see all our things packed into the car, as though we were moving. I didn't know what to say to her, and then she didn't say anything for a long time. But Julia was listening to my mom talking about not being able to look after me anymore. She kept looking at me, and I could see she was really sad about something. We began to whisper things about places we had stayed and what we liked and didn't like. But it was only when we reached town and found the trailer park that Julia whispered the most important thing. *I was taken from my dad two years ago. I shouldn't be with my mom.* We were alone in the car while our moms were in the park office, paying for the campers. At first I thought she was telling me a story. But when I knew she really was in trouble, I didn't know how to help."

"What about her dad? Wasn't he already looking for her?"

"Probably. But he was working in different places, and Julia couldn't remember his phone number. She said to me that her mom's parents met up with them a few times in different places. She thinks they were helping her mom keep her. They were coming to pick up the car after it broke down. They would get it fixed and back to Julia's mom so they could leave again." Bon stopped drawing. "Julia's mom got jobs here and there, stuff like cleaning hotel rooms or doing dishes in places. And if people asked, she'd tell them Julia was being homeschooled. Julia didn't get much of a chance to be with other people. But once she was in our car, once she got here, she was tired of being a scared little kid who did everything her mom told her. She wanted to come to school again. She bought herself the bike."

"I was there," I said. "At the garage sale where she found it."

"Julia got into really big trouble," Bon said, "because she'd gone off for a walk without her mom knowing, and then come back riding a bike that she'd paid for with money from her mom's purse. Her mom got really mad. She dragged Julia into their camper at the trailer park." Bon paused and took a deep breath. "I heard them arguing about it. Julia's mom hated that bike, the same as she hated Julia being at school. She didn't want her talking to anyone. Except Julia had already been talking to me. And finally she told Mrs. Gallagher what her mom had done. So now," Bon said, his voice quietly pleased, "Julia is back with her dad. Her mom would have had a good, *bad* surprise when the police came to visit. I'm glad about that part. I'm glad her dad found her, too." His shoulders dropped and he added, "But not that Julia has gone. I liked how we talked to each other. I miss that."

Bon looked at his drawing. I watched him write a sentence beneath his picture, his scrawly writing clearer somehow. Was I getting used to reading it? *The forces of evil were overwhelmed and life in the town gradually returned to normal.*

My arm and elbow were on the table. I laid my head down and looked sideways at the library and at Bon as he drew. "Have you drawn any inventions lately?" I asked.

Bon closed his book. "Not for a while."

"Why?"

"I don't know. The one new thing I thought of I haven't figured out how to draw yet."

"What is it?"

He took a breath. "It's like ... GPS, except to find people—or to find just one person. You key in their details—their name, age, appearance, last known address—and the person finder tells you where to locate them, where they've moved to." After explaining it to me in an almost-too-quick voice, Bon stopped himself and looked away, embarrassed. "Something like that, anyway."

I waited. "To find Julia?" I asked. To myself I thought, *And Connor.*

"Yes," he said, looking back at his picture. "And Sam. I would use it to find him as well."

I sat up again, remembering who he meant, the person who had once been my aunt's boyfriend—the only one Bon had liked, as far as I could tell. "Why?" I asked.

"Because he was nice. Because I did drawings for him when I was little, and he always said how good they were." Bon slapped his book shut and then reopened it at the first page. "Because he gave me this."

In the background, I heard the bell ringing for the

end of lunchtime recess. Bon pointed at the inside front cover. In all the times I had snuck looks at whatever Bon was drawing, I had never taken much notice of this part of the book. I saw an adult's neat writing, which Bon traced a finger gently across. "There," he said softly, and I followed the path of his finger, silently reading.

To Bon — be brave and determined, nurture your talent, draw your dreams. Sam Irvine.

"Are you two staying the night?" Ms. Tabor called across to us, because suddenly we were the last kids left in the library, and now we were going to be late to our class lines.

"When did Sam give you this?" I asked.

"When I was seven. But I didn't start drawing in it until I was nearly nine." Bon paused. "After I visited your house, that time it was your dad's birthday party. When I saw the toy castle in your bedroom, I knew what sort of pictures I had to draw. And when I met Julia, I knew what sort of story I had to tell."

Bon's mom called.

It was me that picked up the phone when it rang in Nan's kitchen, and my *hello* was met with a moment of weird silence. And then came her voice: "Is that you, Bon?"

"No," I replied. I could feel the shock waves in my voice. "It's me, Aunt Renee. Kieran."

"Oh . . ." Another silence. "Is Bon there at the moment?"

"He's outside. He and Nan are getting the laundry in. It's going to rain soon."

"I guess you think . . ." she began, and I could hear her take a deep breath before she continued. "I guess you think I'm a pretty bad parent."

"No. No, I don't. Aunt Renee?"

"Yes?"

"Are you coming to visit Bon?"

"I don't know. Do you think he'd like to see me?"

"Yes. I think he'd like that a lot."

There was another silence. I realized I was walking in small circles around the kitchen floor, and I nervously wondered what I could say next. "Would you like me to go get Bon for you?"

"Yes. And Kieran . . . ?"

"Yes?"

"Thank you."

I went outside and swapped places with Bon, and in the minutes afterward, I glanced up at the kitchen window once or twice to see how the phone call might be going. Bon wasn't walking in nervous circles like I had been; he stood quite still at the kitchen window—watching us, but talking with his mom.

I looked at Nan, who said, "It's good she called. She needs to do it more regularly." She smiled to herself then, and she reached for the last clothespinned shirt on the line. It gave me time to wonder that my aunt had actually called me by my name, that she had done the same for Bon. That she sounded calm. And that *thank you* might have been for more than simply fetching Bon inside.

Bon tapped the window glass, pointing at the phone and then at Nan, who left me to carry the laundry basket upstairs. I came inside in time to hear her say to my aunt, "But don't hesitate to give Bon a call more often. He hasn't heard from you in more than a month. He needs to hear from you at regular intervals, and he needs to see you, too. We all do."

It was enough for me to know from Nan afterward that Aunt Renee was out of state again, that she was sharing a house with friends and had found a part-time job. And that, yes, she would drive up to visit Bon if she could take time away from work. I didn't want to ask Nan about whether Aunt Renee was taking her medication, but I wondered whether it was making things different for her.

"Are you OK?" Nan asked Bon afterward.

"Yes," he answered. His voice seemed calm and matter-of-fact, and I couldn't tell whether he was happy or sad about the phone call. I couldn't tell whether he missed his mom or not, and I even worried a little that he was wishing to be with her, rather than here with us. "I might go do some drawing and writing," he simply said, and spent a long while that afternoon by himself with his book of maps and inventions.

I waited until much later to ask him. I waited until the quiet part of the evening when we were both in the room that had been for sleepovers, that was now Bon's bedroom. I was still getting used to this different shape of things. There was still the set of shelves with the old books and toys, but there were new things crowded onto them as well, things that Nan and my mom had bought for Bon—books, a large set of drawing pens and a pad of real art paper, a new desk, a chair, and a large bulletin board, where some of Bon's artwork was already hung. His class photo was there, too, and it was easy to spot Julia and Bon, their smiling faces.

"Was it good hearing from your mom?" I asked.

Bon lay on his tummy on the bed, drawing and writing. "Yes," he replied, without looking up.

I was curious and persistent. "Did she tell you where she was and what she was doing, and everything?"

Bon nodded. "About her job, the rental house, about visiting. And," he added with a sigh, "she told me she missed me."

The way he said it worried me. "Don't you believe her?"

"I believe her."

"Do you miss her?" I had wanted to ask that for more than a while.

"A bit. Yes." His voice drifted a little, and then he said, "Most of all, I'd just like her to be happy."

My space at Nan's was now a mattress on the floor near Bon's bed, and after sitting up on it to ask Bon about the phone call, I lay back and stared up at the ceiling, taking a few moments to think of something that might make Bon talk some more. Once, it had been as though he barely knew how to speak, but now I knew that he was full of stories and things to say. I looked across to the chest of drawers and saw a photo of Bon with his mom. It wasn't a recent photo; they were both a bit younger. Bon's hair was strangely shorter and sat on his head differently, and his mom was smiling in a way that somehow didn't quite show *happy*. I tried for a moment to read what that smile could mean. She wore the same jewelry that I remembered her with at Dad's party all that time ago.

Bon said it again, his voice soft and distant. "Most of all, I just want her to be happy."

"What was it like moving around all the time and going to different schools?"

"Sometimes I didn't go to school at all," Bon replied. "It was just me and my mom. Nothing to do and no one else to talk to. So I don't miss moving around and living in different places. I don't miss that at all."

I decided to tell Bon a kind of story as well. "That time you visited us, that time with your mom and that guy in the big black pickup, when you left, Nan was nearly crying."

"Was she?" Bon's pen stopped writing, and he looked down at me.

"Yes. She hadn't seen you for so long and she didn't know when she was going to see you again. When the pickup drove away, it was only you that turned and looked back at us. I still remember that. You kept looking, all the way down the road, until the pickup turned the corner and was gone. Until *you* were gone."

Bon didn't say anything for a while. His eyes were perfectly still, but I could see that he was thinking or remembering.

At last, he said, "Because I wanted to stay. I wanted to *live* here. Now I do." His eyes met mine again. "I'm sorry I touched your toys that time, and messed up your room."

Suddenly, that part seemed so distant and unimportant. "It's OK," I said. "Gina's bedroom looks like that *all* the time."

"I'm sorry I took your things," he said.

I shrugged a reply that I hoped meant, *Don't worry about it.* But I began to think about my medieval castle and its army of little people and horses. I thought about all the times I had played with them, had imagined the castle in a real landscape, and had imagined the voices of the wizard, the royal family, and the knights on horseback. I thought about what Bon had taken, and then about the pictures he had drawn, the story he had written to bring us together in his own imagination.

Bon the Crusader, Julia the Fair, and Kieran the Brave had traveled together and alone in pictures and in Bon's scribbled handwriting. I wondered how that story was going to end.

"Nan gave me that castle for my eighth birthday," I told him at last. "There was a movie about castles, knights, and wizards that I used to watch over and over. I had a birthday party with kids from school. And somehow, Connor—" I stopped. It was still hard to say his name, and I had to think what to say next.

"Your best friend," Bon said. "I remember."

"Out of all the kids I invited, Connor guessed the right kind of gift. He bought me a set of horses and knights that matched the other figures Nan had bought to go with the castle."

"Oh."

I knew Bon was still feeling guilty about the stealing. I remembered how he had come to our town and come to us with no toys of his own. I added, "I don't mind if you play with the castle whenever you stay at our place. Actually, I don't play with it much anymore."

Bon blinked and frowned a little, as though I were making no sense.

"It's OK," I reassured him.

He hesitated and then nodded. "Thank you." Then he said, "You're smiling, Kieran. Why are you smiling?"

He used the serious, precise voice I hadn't heard in a while. "I've never seen you smile like that before."

I changed the subject. "What have you written? What have you drawn?"

Bon hesitated. "Here," he said, turning the open book to me so that I could see. Two knights stood at a high castle parapet that overlooked a village of tiny, crowded houses. They looked toward a far horizon with mountains the shape of those around our own town. And in that distance, two figures on horseback rode away toward the very edges of the picture. Underneath, Bon had written, *And so Julia the Fair was reunited with her true parent. Bon the Crusader and Kieran the Brave returned safe to their castle, ready for whatever challenges lay ahead.*

I nodded. "Is the story finished?"

"Not quite," Bon replied. "But almost." Suddenly, his eyes were wet and he wiped at them with the back of one hand. He closed the book and held it to his chest.

I woke quite early the next morning, just as the room began to brighten with daylight. Bon was up in his bed, asleep. I didn't mind sleeping on the spare mattress down on the floor. It made the room taller and larger from where I lay, and it somehow made me feel younger and smaller. When I listened closely, I could hear Bon's slow, steady sleep breathing. His head was buried under his blankets, and only his braid showed, trailing almost over the edge of the bed.

I crept out to the kitchen. Nan was already at the table with a mug of tea and the morning newspaper. Bon's wool hat lay at the end of the table.

"You're awake!" she exclaimed. "What about Bon?"

I shook my head and sat down opposite her.

"He sleeps a lot better lately," she said, quietly pleased. "Not so much waking up at night or standing out here at two in the morning, staring out the window and scaring me witless." She paused. "Maybe it's a sign that he's content. That he feels safe. That's a thought I rather like."

"He misses his friend Julia," I said.

"I know," Nan replied. "You went through the same thing when your friend Connor left. So you understand how it is for Bon. And you can be there to help him."

The purple bike was propped up on the back porch, and Nan pointed to it. "He's very excited to own her bike. It's a special thing for Bon to have that, thanks to your father tracking it down. I think that fellow at the trailer park was hoping to keep it for himself."

I gazed out the window at the bike that had been Julia's, and then at Nan's garden and the view beyond of the town. I was silent long enough for Nan to finally ask, "Are you OK, Kieran?"

"I feel different," I said, knowing how lost my voice sounded.

"How?"

"I don't know. Just different."

Nan looked at me for a while and then answered, "Well, you don't look any different. Or sound any different." She watched me from above the brim of her mug and took a long sip. Then she asked gently, "Does it feel different in your head and heart, Kieran?"

I shrugged and then nodded.

"A lot has happened in a pretty short time, and a lot has changed. Life is a little different for all of us. It can take a while to get used to things changing. Are you bothered about Bon living here?"

I shook my head. "No, I think it's good." My eyes found the magnetic picture frame on the fridge door. It had three new photos in it now: this year's school photos of Gina, Bon, and me. "It's *really* good," I added. I reached over and picked up Bon's wool hat.

"I gave that a wash," Nan said. "Perhaps the first wash it's had in a very long time."

I slipped a hand inside the hat and turned it around a bit, so that the pom-poms waved and jiggled.

"It's hand knit," Nan said. "I thought at first it was

probably from a thrift shop, like everything Bon came to us wearing. But there's a name inside. He said someone gave it to him."

"Who?" I asked, turning the cap over and searching. There was a little name tag stitched on the inside along a seam. It read SAM IRVINE.

"Someone *did* give it to him," I said. "Someone important." And I told Nan what I knew about a man named Sam who had taught Bon to swim, who had given him his book of maps and inventions, and who had written that special message to Bon about writing and drawing his dreams. Sam, who Bon remembered so well and wanted to find, using one of his crazy inventions. "Is there any way we can find Sam Irvine?" I asked.

Nan thought about it and nodded. "There may be. Anything can be possible using a computer. And," she added with a sigh, "if I pick the right moment, I could try asking Renee. She may be able to help. What do you think?"

"I think we should try to find him. I think it would make Bon very happy."

"Good morning, my dear," Nan said suddenly and brightly, and there was a sleepy-eyed, hair-frizzed Bon in the kitchen doorway. I sensed that he had been there for a while and had heard every word.

I counted down the days till Saturday, till the moment I woke up under the darkness and warmth of my blanket and heard the clock radio in my parents' bedroom explode into talkative life. Two weeks of being grounded was over.

I could hear Gina's footsteps in the hallway as she thumped out to the living room TV and the early-morning cartoons. I could hear Dad's voice, doors opening and closing, and the waterfall crash of the bathroom shower that would fully wake him up. Today was his soccer game, in the last season he said he might ever play. And today, Bon and I were allowed to ride our bikes again.

Bon was awake. His arms stretched straight out from under the covers and then bent to rub his eyes. He looked up at the ceiling, and then across at me. When he smiled, I knew he'd also remembered that today meant no more being grounded.

"Me and Bon," I told Mom as we crunched mouthfuls of toast, "we're going to ride to Dad's game today."

"Pardon?"

"We're riding our bikes. We'll meet you there."

In that instant her face had gone from calm to serious. "What makes you think you're doing that?"

"The two weeks are over, Mom. We're not grounded anymore. Two weeks, you said. And today's the day after two weeks."

She glanced over at the calendar on the fridge door and saw that I was right. "Ah, yes," she said slowly, stretching the words out like elastic.

"We'll be OK. We'll go straight there."

"We *promise*," Bon added.

"I'll be OK. *We'll* be OK. We don't want to be driven everywhere forever until we're grown-ups."

"But we're talking out of town, Kieran. It's three miles. Bon might not have your experience when it comes to bike riding."

"Mom, it's easy. There's a bike path some of the way. You can drive back and make sure we're OK."

Her look told me I'd gone a little too far. "I don't want to check up on you," she said. "I just want to know that you'll get there safely. Will you be able to ride that far, Bon? "

Bon nodded happily. "I'll be OK. I'm a better rider than I used to be."

I heard the *clunk* of Dad's gym bag as he dropped it by the front door.

"These two want to ride their bikes out to the soccer field," she told him.

Dad, whose head had probably been full of soccer-match thoughts, looked a bit stunned at first. "Ride? Bikes?"

"We're not grounded as of today," I reminded him.

"Oh, yes," he said, remembering. It came out as *Ooooohhhh, yeeeesssss,* in the same elastic voice as Mom's. He glanced at her for a moment, then said to us, "Trust. That's what it's going to be about from now on: trust. No more running off by yourselves." He looked at Bon. "Or your*self.* You both show us you can do the right thing. You look out for each other from now on."

"We know," I groaned. *"Dad."*

"You ride straight there," Mom added. "No stopping at the store, no sidetracking. *Straight* to the soccer field. Promise?"

"We promise," we chorused. It sounded funny, our voices saying the same thing at the same time. My parents were making it sound like we were about to go on a bike ride around the planet, instead of just down to the local soccer field.

Mom always did the driving on game days. As she put her seat belt on and clicked the car into gear, she told me, "I expect you there by ten o'clock. Don't be late and do be careful."

Dad leaned across from the other seat and said, "The Locomotives are going to kick some backsides today! How could you miss that?" And he winked, adding, "See you at the game, boys."

Gina was not impressed. "Why can't I ride my bike, too? It isn't fair."

"When you're older," Mom reassured her.

"I *am* older," Gina grumbled. "I used to be five and now I'm six."

As the car backed out of the driveway, I could still hear my sister from the backseat: "It isn't fair. I'm getting older *all* the time. "

"All *right*," I murmured as our car turned the corner at the end of our street. They'd be at the soccer field in a matter of minutes, in time to watch the reserve-team game and for Dad to get together with his team, discuss strategies, and do warm-ups.

But I didn't want to race there just to keep Mom calm. I decided to take it easy and enjoy my first and biggest bike ride in ages. Besides, I had Bon to think of as well. In the first moments, he was a bit awkward on his purple bike, wobbling a little, still getting used to gears and brakes. I let him go a short way by himself, and then caught up so that I was leading, with him close behind.

We cycled lazily. There was the gentle downhill slope from our house to the corner, and then the flat surface of Sheridan Street ahead. It was a cold morning, good for bike riding and, later on, good for cheering and jumping up and down at a soccer game. Our breath came out in little puffs of mist. The shops were beginning to open now, and cars were parked along the roadside. There were a few people out. Everything felt safe and familiar.

As we left the shops behind, I could hear a chorus of voices across the rooftops. "That's the reserve team's game starting," I told Bon. "We've got lots of time yet."

We came to Mountford Road, a place of workshops and factories. At this edge of town were the auto junkyards and a long, straight stretch of road that passed fields of cows and horses. It was where the bike path began.

Mom and Dad and Gina would be there by now. I could picture their car journey in my head: by Mountford Road, Dad would have gone quiet, concentrating on the game to be played. Mom would be saying something about the weather or the friends she'd see. And in the backseat, Gina would be staring out the window and possibly still complaining. As Mom drove into the parking lot, Dad would be taking his earring out and putting it in the tray beside the handbrake. With the car stopped and switched off, Gina would reach forward and hug Dad around the neck, saying, "Go, Dad. You'll win. I know you will!" Then he and Mom would lean across and kiss each other, and Mom would say, "Have a good game. Good luck. We're there for you."

Dad would pick up his gym bag to stride off to the changing rooms and—

My quiet thoughts were interrupted by a chorus of cheers that drifted to us from the direction of the sports field, and I guessed that someone had just scored a goal. The bike path swung away to one side of the road and passed under low trees and alongside a field where cows grazed in the distance. There was a little bridge over a creek, where Bon slowed his bike to gaze at the ripple of water that washed over stones and a blackened log. I could hear the click and rattle of his bike as he caught up to me again, and quickly, we glanced at each other. I could tell he was enjoying himself. It didn't take any conversation to know that.

We came to the soccer field and the meandering rows of parked cars. Someone had the fund-raiser food stand going, and the smell of onions, bacon, and pancakes drifted through the air to us. We came to the boundary fence and began to walk our bikes.

It didn't take long to find Mom and Gina in the sideline crowd.

"Good ride?" Mom asked.

"It was great," I said cheerfully. "I've missed bike riding a lot."

"Me, too," added Bon, and immediately looked embarrassed.

Gina pouted. "I wish I could ride *my* bike to the game like the boys were allowed to."

"I'm hungry," Bon announced.

Mom gave us each some money, and we laid our bikes on the grass behind where she and Gina had set up their folding chairs, and we set off toward the food stand. My dad's game would start in a little while, and I could see him now, sitting with his teammates under a shade awning down at the end of the sideline, too far away for me to catch his attention with a wave. I thought of walking over to say *hello* and *good luck*. Had he meant what he'd said in the park that early morning? I just didn't want to think of today as being one of the last times Dad would jog onto a field with

225

his team. We wouldn't be able to cheer for him from the sidelines anymore, and I knew the thought of him coaching one of the junior teams would take a long time for me to get used to.

There were plenty of the usual familiar faces in the crowd around us—people I recognized from town and people who had visited our house for parties and barbecues. And there were the unfamiliar faces and voices of strangers, a lot of them wearing the colors of the opposing team.

We bought a warm breakfast snack each. I was finished in a couple of mouthfuls, and then had to wait in silence for Bon to finish.

"Let's climb the hill," he said, his mouth still half full.

"What?"

"The hill. I know where the path is. Have you ever climbed it before?"

"Sure I have. But—" I looked anxiously at my watch. "I want to be here when Dad's game starts."

"There's enough time to walk up the path and then come down again," Bon replied.

"But today's important," I reminded him. "This might be one of Dad's last games, and I don't want to miss anything."

"The hill's important, too." Bon said.

I squinted at him. "Important? What are you talking about?"

"It just is. We can be quick."

"OK," I agreed reluctantly. "But I have to talk to Dad first. Wait over at the fence." I zigzagged through the crowd to where the team sat under the shade canopy. Ant was telling a joke. Split Pin was doing knee bends and stretches. Dad had already done some warm-ups and was sitting quietly, his face glazed with perspiration. He didn't notice me wandering over until I tapped him on the shoulder.

"Hey, buddy," he said, ruffling my hair. "You made it. You didn't lose Bon, did you?"

"No, he's here."

"It'll do him good to get out a bit, ride a bike like you can. So make sure you guys don't get yourselves grounded again, eh? Next thing we know, we'll have him kicking a ball around! What do you think?"

"Yeah," I said, a little amused by the thought. "That'd be good. Dad?"

"Yes, pal?"

"Good luck. Have a good game."

He raised his eyebrows and nodded. "I will. We will. It's our game today." He paused and then added, "Go on, you'd better get back to your mom. I need my cheering squad—all four of you."

Four? I immediately wondered, but then it dawned on me. Of course he'd included Bon.

I climbed back under the sideline fence. In just those few moments, more people had crowded along the edges of the field. I looked across to where Mom and Gina were, and then to where I could see Bon waiting at the fence beside the parking lot. He waved a hand and then set off toward where the path to the lookout began. I ran to catch up.

"Bon, we have to be quick. I don't want to be late for Dad's game."

"It's OK; we won't be long."

"It's a steep climb," I warned.

"I know," he replied, leaving the last patch of grass and heading to where the path began to snake through the undergrowth.

I followed him. The lookout was simply a clearing and a large rock on the bushy hill behind the soccer field, but I knew the whole town could be seen. The first few minutes of walking and climbing were the hardest—the trail was steep and dusty, and there were empty cans and scraps of trash on the ground along the way. Not quite at the top of the hill was a gap in the trees where the boulder sat, large and round. Climbing up onto it the wrong way meant broken fingernails and scraped skin. My forehead was sweaty and I gulped air, but the climb had seemed like nothing to Bon, and I was surprised by his burst of energy. While I squatted down for a moment to catch my breath and wipe my face across my sleeve, Bon found his way up onto the boulder. He stood uneasily and a bit off-balance before sitting himself down.

"Have you been up on top here before?" he asked.

I nodded. "Ages ago. With Mason and Lucas."

"Oh," he said.

I climbed up onto the boulder and sat down as well. "Look, there's the whole town," I remarked, waving an arm at the colored roofs of the Sheridan Street shops, the lines of streets, and the boxy houses scattered like sprinkles on a cake. "And that big silver-and-red roof—that's Rural Engineering, where Dad works."

"You can see the road out of town," Bon said. "It loops from north to south and joins the highway *there*." He pointed and traced a finger from left to right. "And *there*."

I tried to find the view he was seeing. And there it was—the ribbons of road and tiny moving traffic, and beyond that, green farm hills and bushy mountains as far as the western horizon. My eyes settled on the highway that vanished into valleys and rode over hills.

I blinked and stared hard at Bon. "You *have* been up here before."

Bon was twirling the end of his braid around his index finger and staring into space. After a pause, he answered, "Yes. With Julia."

"When?"

Bon sighed. "On a Saturday once. It was a game day." He pointed down the slope. "Just like today. I saw you with Gina and your parents, and I saw your dad score a goal. Julia had her bike, and she was teaching me how to ride it. We took turns, all the way out of town."

"How did you and Julia know about the trail up here?"

"From kids at school. We climbed up here and looked around. We talked." Bon let go of his braid and looked at me. It was different from his usual sideways gaze. Without waiting for the question I was bound to ask next, he continued. "We talked about what it would be like to leave. To go away and travel by ourselves."

"Where to?" And I could have added, *How?*

"Everywhere. Jungles, rivers, snowfields, deserts. Other countries, all the places we'd seen in books and on documentaries. We looked at the atlas maps in the library at school as well." He paused, and then added dreamily, "I like maps."

"But you're still a kid," I told him. "So's Julia. How would you do all that by yourselves?"

"We used our imaginations." Bon's voice strayed, just for a moment, back into being odd and precise. "We knew we could really travel together one day. Once we're adults."

I thought about that for a moment. Feeling brave, I said, "I miss her. She was smart; she was nice; she was *different*. I just wish she hadn't gone."

A breeze started above our heads and made the leaves in the trees sway and clatter. Something made me start to think of this hill as Julia's hiding place, or a place that somehow hid her. I wondered where she was now.

"Why did you want us to climb up here?" I asked. "It's like there's a special reason. Please, tell me, Bon."

Bon was silent long enough for me to think of another time that was only weeks ago, but now seemed as distant as photos in an album. I knew I had treated him badly. I knew I had thought of him as being strange, unlikeable, and weak.

His hand held my shoulder tightly, and I was surprised at the strength and confidence in his voice as well. He took a deep breath. "Like I told you—we talked about . . . *stuff*, about each other and about our families. And the way we felt. We were friends." He paused. "I know you liked her. I know you wanted to be friends with her, too."

"I'm sorry," I said. "About Julia leaving. She was your best friend."

"I'd never had a best friend before," Bon replied. "And my *first* best friend was a girl." He leaned on the word *first,* as though he were going to announce *second* as well. Except he didn't. He simply smiled at me.

"Do you know where Julia is now?" I asked, sensing that Bon did know.

"Her dad works on a fishing boat, way down south. So that's where Julia is—with him at home, or waiting for him to come home from work."

How do you know? I was about to ask, but a sudden noise of cheering and clapping echoed up through the bushes. I checked my watch and knew that Dad's team had jogged onto the field, that the game was about to begin.

"Bon, we need to go back," I said, feeling worried, but guessing that our time up here was not quite over. Because now I knew almost everything Bon knew. And he had become, by a process I didn't yet completely understand, something more than my cousin. For a moment, I tried to imagine that I was up here on the hill by myself, that Bon was not beside me and had never arrived in our town. In this other short imagining, I was still trying to be best friends with Mason and Lucas. I was still trying to be popular. But now I could see that I had been quite alone. I turned to Bon, looked into his eyes, and tried to read his thoughts a little, thinking of that time at my dad's birthday party.

We're brothers, we are.

That moment had never left me, the year that Bon and I had turned nine. Now, in the year that we had both turned eleven, I caught the fragrances of shampoo in his hair and laundry soap in his clothes. They were the smells of Nan's house and ours, of our family.

"Before we go back, there's something I have to show you." Bon leaned to one side and pulled something from his back pocket. "It was in Nan's mailbox yesterday afternoon when I got home from school. I saved it for today. For up here, where it's like you can nearly see the whole world," he told me. "It's to both of us. You'll feel happy. *I* felt happy when I got it. There's an address on it that we can write back to."

In his hand, he held what looked like a photo, but I realized it was a postcard. The front showed a beach landscape of pale sand and dry green hills behind the shape of a distant lighthouse. Bon smiled warmly and turned the postcard over.

Bon's name and Nan's address were in large penned

233

letters on the back. Next to it was a written note—
a girl's handwriting, with *j*'s that looped and *a*'s and *e*'s
that curled at the ends.

Dear Bon and Kieran, it began. As Bon handed it to
me, he leaned against me a little, the way he did with
Nan and Mom.

Slowly, I took the postcard from his hand and began
reading.

DISCARDED